For Many
Shall Come
in My Name

For Many Shall Come in My Name

How the "ancient wisdom" is drawing millions of people into mystical experiences and preparing the world for the end of the age

Ray Yungen

Expanded 2nd Edition
Lighthouse Trails Publishing
Eureka, Montana, USA

For Many Shall Come in My Name

© 2007 Ray Yungen
2nd Edition 2007, 5th printing 2013
Lighthouse Trails Publishing
P.O. Box 908
Eureka, Montana 59917
www.lighthousetrails.com

First edition published in 1991 by Solid Rock Books.

Scripture quotations are taken from the *King James Version.*

Lighthouse Trails books are available at special quantity discounts. Contact information for publisher in back of book.

═══

Library of Congress Cataloging-in-Publication Data

Yungen, Ray.
For many shall come in my name / Ray Yungen. — 2nd ed.
    p. cm.
Includes bibliographical references (p.   ) and index.
ISBN-13: 978-0-9721512-9-0 (softbound : alk. paper)
1. New Age movement. 2. Christianity and other religions—New
Age movement. I. Title.
BP605.N48Y98 2006
239'.93—dc22
                            2006023085

Printed in the United States of America

To Mary and Alberto,
whose conference in 1984
set me on this path

Contents

"And he [Jesus] said, Take heed that ye be not deceived: for many shall come in my name, saying, I am Christ; and the time draweth near: go ye not therefore after them." (Luke 21:8)

INTRODUCTION

I first became aware of what is called the New Age movement in 1984. At first, it sounded like something only hippies and East Indian gurus practiced. But the more I read about it, the more my curiosity and interest grew. I combed through health food stores and New Age book stores looking through books, pamphlets, and magazines. I soon realized the New Age movement was something that had greatly impacted society, and its influence was growing rapidly.

It wasn't long before I encountered detractors who thought I was wasting my time, or worse, delving into areas which had the potential to be dangerous. Despite this criticism, I remained staunchly convinced of the validity of my pursuit. I examined my motives and seriously considered whether the research I was doing was legitimate. After much self-examination, I concluded that my research should continue because what I was doing would someday benefit other people (New Agers very much included). Many shocking, progressive revelations occurred over the next few years—society was indeed being affected on a grand scale.

Those early years of research had a beneficial side effect. They sparked in me a deeper spiritual interest, which seems logical when one considers the implications of the New Age movement.

I had been a believing Christian since the age of nine, but for the most part I had been a passive, worldly one rather than one who "earnestly contends for the faith." I knew a few Bible verses and was not greatly committed to learning more. I always felt convicted about my apathy but never acted on that conviction. However, when I began to realize the New Age movement was actually fulfilling biblical prophecy, my faith was stirred, and I was convicted to act. How could I continue to remain indifferent?

I began compiling my research and speaking to small groups of interested people. At the suggestion of various friends and acquaintances, I turned the research into a book. With a small publisher who is now defunct, the first edition of *For Many Shall Come in My Name* was released in 1991.

Much of the material from that first edition is within the pages of this new expanded edition, as it remains relevant and is an accurate gauge of what is happening in our society. But because the intensity of the New Age movement has accelerated, partly due to the Internet and increased communication technology, this new edition is crucial. Few people anymore are not affected by the New Age. Its influence is found in medicine, business, education, the media, and religion.

I have written this book so those who read it will gain a clear understanding of what the New Age movement entails and how it is impacting nearly every family in some way. Even more so, I hope *For Many Shall Come in My Name* will connect the dots and give a portrait of the implications of this powerful, yet often obscure, movement.

Ray Yungen

ONE

WHAT IS THE NEW AGE?

M Y first exposure to what I later came to know as the New Age movement was in 1974 when I moved to Berkeley, California, to attend a film institute. From the first day I arrived, I found "Berserkeley" (as it was nicknamed) a fascinating and exotic town, a place unlike any I had ever seen. The town surged with a rebellious, wacky vitality. It has been said of Berkeley that the strange and the odd are ordinary and the conventional out of place.

Berkeley had a notorious reputation as a hotbed of student protest dating from the Free Speech movement in 1964. I lived only a few blocks from the vacant lot called "People's Park," which was the scene of bloody clashes between police, street people, and students in 1969. Militant Leftist rhetoric and literature were evident everywhere. Telephone poles displayed various manifestos and communiques from groups with formidable sounding names such as "the People's Revolutionary Underground Red Guerrilla Commune." Pictures of Chairman Mao and Karl Marx decorated the walls of several co-op health food stores.

There was also a very open and prevalent drug culture. Smoking pot in public was so common that many took it for granted. I was familiar with the drug culture and radical politics through personal exposure and the media, but it soon became apparent something else was happening in Berkeley that I had not encountered before.

Berkeley and its Unfamiliar Terminology

Many unfamiliar terms began to catch my attention. I met people who talked about such things as *karma* and *exploring inner space*. I frequently heard the words *Aquarius* and *Aquarian*, and it was commonplace to ask about a person's zodiac sign.

I noticed that many of those using these terms were not burned-out street people but rather the articulate and well-educated. Their unusual spiritual outlook intrigued me, but I passed it off as the eccentricity associated with Berkeley and the San Francisco Bay area. Had someone told me this *Aquarian consciousness* would someday spread through every facet of Western society, I would have thought him as crazy as the wild-looking street people hanging around the periphery of the University of California.

While living in the Berkeley Film House I became friends with Brian, a young man from the East Coast. Brian was personable, intelligent, and witty. With both of us being avid film buffs, we enjoyed many good times together discussing the cinema and even made plans to collaborate on a film someday. After I had completed my film courses, Brian offered to drive me home to Oregon in his rattletrap Volkswagen bug so he could check out the beauty of the Northwest. Eventually he settled in a city near my hometown, enabling us to keep in touch.

During our visits, Brian often talked about subjects he termed *spiritual* or *holistic*. Often he spoke about Christ or *Christ consciousness* and the world peace and brotherhood which would eventually be achieved though this. It all sounded very positive.

Each time these sermons took place, I wondered just what it was he was trying to convey. The words he used were familiar, but the meanings he attached to them were peculiar and out of place. The exchanges I had with Brian were very frustrating at times.

Whenever I tried to present a more traditional Christian viewpoint on spiritual matters, he would become highly irritated and respond with, "The Bible is nothing but metaphor to show deeper spiritual truths" or "The churches have completely missed the real meaning of Jesus' teachings and have substituted rigid rules and dogma to control people instead." Brian was adamant on this belief.

What perplexed me was how Brian had developed these spiritual ideas, which he had tried so hard to make me understand. He didn't belong to a cult or anything of that sort. I wondered where these ideas came from. I would ask him, "Brian, what *is* this?" He would shoot back, "You can't label truth."

Although I didn't see it clearly at the time, Brian's spiritual outlook was a mixture of what he referred to as, "All the world's great spiritual traditions and paths." He talked about Jesus and often quoted from the Bible, yet he had a little shrine in his apartment to the Hindu mystic and saint Sri Ramakrishna. He genuinely felt there was *no difference* between the teachings of Jesus and Ramakrishna. "The great masters all taught the same thing—the kingdom of God is *within*," he would declare with great conviction.

What is the New Age Movement?

In the last few decades, a curious spiritual movement has increasingly made itself known in the Western world. It is referred to by many as the New Age movement. As I will show through this book, its influence has come out into the open and moved into the mainstream of society. One New Age writer predicted it quite accurately when he observed the following in 1985:

It has probably been going on for decades—probably,
by some people's definitions, for centuries—and yet
there can be no denying that it has now taken on
a new sense of exponential growth that suggests it
could well touch the lives of everyone on the planet
by the year 2000.[1]

And right he was! By the beginning of the new millennium,
this is exactly what has happened.

It is important to understand that the term *New Age* is
not widely used by its adherents anymore, but for the sake of
clarity, I shall use this term to identify both practitioners and
the movement itself. I am convinced that this spirituality has
significantly impacted the lives of the majority of the population
today, regardless of class or ethnic background. By the time you
finish this book, I believe you will concur with my conclusions.

An accurate definition of the New Age movement would
be: Individuals who, in the context of historical occultism, are in
mystical contact with unseen sources and dimensions; who receive
guidance and direction from these dimensions, and most impor-
tantly, who *promote* this state-of-being to the rest of humanity.

It is extremely difficult to understand this movement without
first understanding the underlying belief systems and practices
that accompany its agenda. Equally necessary is an understanding of where these beliefs and practices originated and how they
have become pervasive.

The Age of Aquarius

The term *New Age* is based on astrology. Those who
believe in astrology believe in cosmic cycles called *Astrological
Ages*, in which earth passes through a cycle or time period when
it is under the influence of a certain sign of the zodiac. These
Ages last approximately 2,000 years, with a *cusp* or transitory
period between each.

Those who embrace astrology say that for the last 2,000 years we have been in the sign of "Pisces" the fish. Now they say we are moving into the sign of "Aquarius" or the *Age of Aquarius,* hence the New Age.

The Aquarian Age is supposed to signify that the human race is now entering a Golden Age. Many occultists have long heralded the Aquarian Age as an event that would be significant to humanity. That is why one New Age writer states:

> [A] basic knowledge of Astrological Ages is of enormous importance in occult work.[2]

They believe that during these transitions certain cosmic influences begin to flow into the mass consciousness of mankind and cause changes to occur in accordance with the spiritual keynote or theme of that particular Age. This phenomenon is known as *planetary transformation*—an event they believe will bring *universal oneness* to all mankind. The view is that as more and more members of the human race *attune* themselves to *Aquarian energies,* the dynamics of the *old age* will begin to fade out.

To just *what* energies are we supposed to attune ourselves? New Age thought teaches that everything that exists, seen or unseen, is made up of energy—tiny particles of vibrating energy, atoms, molecules, protons, etc. All is energy. That energy, they believe, is God, and therefore, *all is God.* They believe that since we are all part of this God-energy, then *we, too, are God.* God is not seen as a Being that dwells in heaven, but as the universe itself. According to one writer, "Simply put, God functions in you, through you, and as you."[3]

The Age of Aquarius is when we are all supposed to come to the *understanding that man is God.* As one New Age writer put it:

> A major theme of Aquarius is that *God is within.* The goal in the Age of Aquarius will be how to bring this idea into *meaningful reality.* (emphasis mine)[4]

Metaphysics

To fully comprehend the above concept, one has to understand its *essence*, which is built on a belief system commonly referred to as *metaphysics*. The word translates as meta—above or beyond, and physical—the seen or material world. So metaphysics relates to that which exists or is real, but is unseen. In the book, *Metaphysics: The Science of Life*, one practitioner describes metaphysics as the existence of "forces and principles that are hidden from the five senses, . . . thus requiring an altered state of consciousness, and consequently, 'known to very few.'"[5]

Although the word *metaphysics* is also used in non-New Age connotations, it is used in reference to the occult arts so often that the two have become interchangeable. From now on, when I use the term *metaphysics*, I am referring to *New Age* metaphysics. Metaphysics concerns itself with the spiritual evolution of the human soul. This is called the *law of rebirth*, more commonly known as *reincarnation*.

Metaphysical proponents teach there is the seen world known as the physical or material plane and the unseen world with its many different planes. They teach the *astral* plane is where people go after death to await their next incarnation or bodily state.

Metaphysical thought holds the view that we are constantly caught up in a cycle of coming from the astral plane, being born, living, dying, and returning to the astral existence. They believe that the reason for repeating this cycle is to learn lessons that are necessary for our evolutionary training.

The earth plane is supposed to be the ultimate school. If a person *flunks* one incarnation, he must make up for it in the next cycle. This is called *the law of karma*. Reincarnation and karma are always linked together as there cannot be one without the other. The end result is: there is no evil, only lessons to learn.

What is the main lesson? That *you* are God. This is *the* basic tenet of metaphysical thought. The ultimate goal in metaphysics is attuning oneself to *higher consciousness* thereby gaining an awareness of these higher worlds or realms. How does one go about *learning* this? How is this perception achieved? According to New Age beliefs, the most direct way to achieve this is through the practice of *meditation*. Meditation is the basic activity that underlies *all* metaphysics and is the primary source of spiritual direction for the New Age person. We need only observe the emphasis that is placed on meditation to see the significance of its role in New Age thought:

> Meditation is the doorway between worlds . . . the pathway between dimensions.[6]

> Meditation is the key—the *indispensable* key—to the highest states of awareness.[7]

> Meditation is a key ingredient to metaphysics, as it is the single most important act in a metaphysicians life.[8]

What exactly *is* meditation? The meditation many of us are familiar with involves a deep, continuous *thinking* about something. But New Age meditation does just the *opposite*. It involves ridding oneself of all thoughts in order to *still* the mind by putting it in pause or neutral. An analogy would be turning a fast-moving stream into a still pond by damming the free flow of water. This is the purpose of New Age meditation. It *holds back* active thought and causes a *shift* in consciousness. The following explanation makes this process very clear:

> One starts by silencing the mind—for many, this is not easy, but when the mind has become silent and still, it is then possible for the Divine Force to descend and enter into the receptive individual. First it trickles in, and later, in it comes in waves. It is both transforming and cleansing; and it is through this force that divine transformation will be achieved.[9]

This condition is not to be confused with daydreaming, where the mind dwells on a particular subject. New Age meditation works differently in that an *object* acts as a holding mechanism until the mind becomes thoughtless, empty—silent.

English mystic Brother Mandus wrote of his adventure into these realms in his book *This Wondrous Way of Life*. He spoke of being "fused in Light," which he described as "the greatest experience in my life" that gave him "Ecstasy transcending anything I could understand or describe."[10]

In order to grasp what this movement really entails the reader must understand what was happening to Brother Mandus. He wasn't merely believing something on the intellectual level, he was undergoing a supernatural transformation. In truth, he had created a mental void through meditation, and a spiritual force had filled it.

The two most common methods used to induce this *thoughtless* state are *breathing exercises*, in which attention is focused on the breath, and a *mantra*, which is a repeated word or phrase. The basic process is to focus and maintain concentration without actually thinking about what is being focused on. Repetition on the focused object triggers the blank mind.

Just consider the word *mantra*. The translation from the Sanskrit is *man*, meaning "to think" and *tra*, meaning "to be liberated from."[11] Thus, the word means *to be freed from thought*. By repeating the mantra, either aloud or silently, the word or phrase begins to lose any meaning it once had. The same is true with rhythmic breathing. One gradually tunes out his conscious thinking process until an altered state of consciousness comes over him.

I recall watching a martial arts class where the instructor clapped his hands once every three seconds as the students sat in meditation. The sound of the clap acted the same as the breath or a mantra would—something to focus their attention on to stop the active mind.

Other methods of meditation involve drumming, dancing, and chanting. This *percussion-sound* meditation is perhaps the most common form for producing trance states in the African,

North/South American Indian, and Brazilian spiritist traditions. In the Islamic world, the Sufi Mystic Brotherhoods have gained a reputation for chanting and ritual dancing. They are known as the *Whirling Dervishes*. The Indian Guru, Rajneesh, developed a form of active meditation called *dynamic meditation*, which combines the percussion sound, jumping, and rhythmic breathing.

The Higher Self

At the very core of the meditation effort is the concept of what is called the *higher self*. This is thought to be the part of the individual linked to the *Divine Essence* of the Universe, the part of man that is God. Contact with this higher self is the ultimate goal in meditation and has always been at the very heart of occultism.

There are many different names for the higher self, including: the *Oversoul, True Self, Real Self, Inner Self, Inner Teacher, Inner Guide, Inner Light, Inner Essence, Inner Source, Inner Healer, Soul-Self, Inner Wisdom, Christ Self Superconscious, Divine Center, Divine Spark, Atman*, and the *Creative/Intuitive Self*. Any name that smacks of some latent source of *inner knowledge* or *mystical power* can be used.

As stated earlier, the goal of meditation is to *subdue* the conscious or active mind so that higher consciousness can enter. The metaphysician believes that if he can connect himself *to* and eventually attune *with* his higher self, this will facilitate the higher self's emergence into the physical plane bringing the person under the guidance and direction of this source. This connection is referred to in New Age circles as *awakening, transformation, enlightenment, Self-realization, Cosmic consciousness, Christ consciousness, nirvana, satori,* and finding *the kingdom within*.

New Agers believe the person has been *asleep* as to who he is and why he is here in light of all of his previous incarnations. Once the person discovers and joins up with his *divine presence*, he *awakens* from his lower-self sleep state. Once a person knows the *truth* about himself, he no longer has to come back to the earth plane anymore. Having learned that he is God, he rises after death into the higher planes as pure spirit, up the cosmic evolutionary ladder where there is no limit to how far he can evolve.

After this state has been reached, this *enlightened* human being can then act as *a spirit guide* for those who have yet to achieve this state by giving them advice while they are in meditative states. When a person merges with the higher self, he is on his way to *empowerment*, meaning he is capable of creating his own reality. Basically, all power is within the higher self, so when one is in tune with it, he can run his own show. Fear of creating bad karma is supposed to keep the practitioner from using this power for evil purposes.

Metaphysicians believe that we all create our own circumstances anyway, so when we are guided and empowered by our higher self, we can consciously *co-create* with it.

The technique used for this is called *creative visualization.* Author Diane Stein explains the link between meditation and visualization in *The Women's Spirituality Book.* She first instructs her readers to do the rhythmic breathing and deep relaxation exercises (meditation), a prerequisite for entering "the receptive state" and "going between the worlds."[12] Stein then gives an example:

> A woman who wishes to hold a seashell in her hand does rhythmic breathing and deep relaxation to put her in a receptive state. Then she visualizes the shell she desires, its shape, texture, what it feels like to hold it, . . . its color and salty odor. If she continues this visualization nightly, she soon finds her seashell. Someone brings it to her from their beach vacation, she sees and buys it at a garage sale or finds it long-forgotten in her own basement. When she sees the shell, she recognizes it immediately as her own, her desire is fulfilled, the thought form transferred from emotional to physical levels, and the object itself drawn to her from between the worlds.[13]

John Randolf Price offers another explanation of how the creative visualization process works in his book, *The Superbeings:*

> While it is true that a new home . . . will not suddenly appear in the back yard of your present dwelling, events and circumstances will take place enabling you to acquire the home you desire.[14]

Meditation and creative visualization definitely accompany one another in this process. As one New Age manual explains:

> Tune in to the Inner Divinity, the Source, the God within, and feel that Presence as you. This first step is essential. If it is incomplete, the rest of the process will not work.[15]

Manifestations

Upon examination of New Age materials, it becomes quite apparent that even though New Age proponents claim that the higher self is *within* each person, there is a *visible presence* as well. These beings can be seen at times, such as the following confirms:

> Your Higher-Self can appear to you in many forms, depending on what you need at a particular time. Some people report experiencing the Higher-Self as specifically male or female. But more often, people report perceiving their Higher-Self as a being of light which seems beyond sexuality—beyond the physical separation between male and female.[16]

Shirley MacLaine described her higher self in the following profound encounter:

> I saw the form of a very tall, overpoweringly confident, almost androgynous human being. A graceful, folded, cream-colored garment flowed over

> a figure seven feet tall, with long arms resting calmly at
> its side. . . . It raised its arms in outstretched welcome.
> . . . It was simple, but so powerful that it seemed to
> "know" all there was to know. . . . "Who are you?"
> I asked. . . . The being smiled at me and embraced
> me! "I am your higher unlimited self," it said.[17]

This reflects the *genie in the lamp* story popularized by cartoons and a television sit-com of the 1960s. Originally, the genie represented the higher self, who was reached through meditation by staring at the flame of an oil lamp. It was believed that a person could have whatever he or she wanted, once in touch with it.

Our word *genius* comes from this Latin word for spirit guide and now means a person with great creative power.

The Ultimate Reality

To review, the New Age concepts of Self-realization are:

- All that exists *is* God.
- All Mankind is part of that divinity.
- In each person, there dwells the higher self, which is the *divine essence* of that person.
- The higher self is the guide to realizing the wisdom of the universe.
- Meditation (stilling the mind of thought) is the way to connect with the higher self.
- A person can control his own reality once he has contacted the higher self, working in unison with its powers.

These fundamental elements are the basis for the New Age. This phenomenon is more than just an intellectual acceptance of *ideas*. There has to be a real power or force involved to give *seeming validity* to these belief structures. To believe one is God one must *first feel* like he or she is God. As one teacher of these practices commented:

We try to help people get in touch with their divine
self or their inner self, whatever one wants to call it.
It's not religious, it's spiritual. It's connecting with
that divine being within yourself or whatever you
want to call it and acknowledging the power you
have, the control you have over your life. You're not
out of control. You are not helpless.[18]

I have often wondered why the *spooky* nature of metaphysics
has not deterred more people from becoming involved in it. I
believe there is a reason for this—its appeal comes from the way
it is presented.

The following incident clearly shows how metaphysics is
viewed by its adherents: I was browsing through a New Age
bookstore with a couple of friends. Before long they began
quietly muttering to each other their disapproval of what they
were seeing. The owner of the store overheard their remarks and
in an incredulous and irritated voice asked them, "What's the
matter, don't you want to *grow?*"

New Agers see what they are involved in as nothing more
than self-development and emancipation from the bonds of life's
frustrations and failures. They believe they are in touch with a
source that will *improve* their lot in life and bring them personal
happiness and well-being.

A perfect example of this viewpoint is found in the spiritual
quest of Celeste Graham. Graham was a remarkably talented
and accomplished young lady. By the age of sixteen, she man-
aged her own record company and magazine and *at* seventeen
went on to have her own publishing house. She also attained
three doctorates and numerous degrees along the way. What she
lacked, though, was a sense of understanding of why she was
here, *and* why all her material accomplishments didn't end her
soul-searching and frustration with life.

Soon Graham became involved with meditation and metaphysics. To fully understand why the New Age movement has

become so popular, we must first understand the sense of elated discovery that is propelling huge numbers in the same direction as Graham when she proclaimed:

> God-conscious awareness, or awakening to our divinity is the ultimate freedom. It opens doors to experiences that are beyond our imagination. It elevates man to his highest estate, frees him from the limitations of the physical, and lifts him up to the divine. It is the purpose of life, the ultimate reality.[19]

This, in a nutshell, is what New Age spirituality is all about. Even though it may be called by many other terms, what Graham described above is the common experience for those who have embraced this spiritual approach and are now promoting it to others. What we are witnessing is unprecedented in human history. Certain conditions have caused this flowering and brought society to a place where it is now open to the New Age like never before. What happened, and how did this phenomenon come to be?

TWO

THE ADVENT OF THE
"ANCIENT WISDOM"

MANY people may think the New Age movement is a collection of strange cults populated by aging hippies, emotional cripples, and assorted oddballs who are duped by money-hungry charlatans and egocentric frauds. This may be true in some instances, but if such were the overall case, I would not have spent the last 22 years researching this movement or writing about my discoveries. The focus of this book is not on fringe religious groups or New Age riff-raff but on a broad-based effort to influence and restructure our whole society.

Rather than creating new institutions as is the case with cults, the New Age goal is to transform people within existing institutions and thereby transform the institutions themselves! As one writer explained it, "...a *new* society forming within the heart of the old."[1]

This transformation has frequently been referred to as a *paradigm shift*. The word paradigm means model, as in outlook or viewpoint.

New Agers predict that as more and more people achieve contact with and guidance from the higher self, a *global shift* will occur, in which the transformed state will become as common as watching television or reading a newspaper. It will be the predominant model or paradigm for humanity.

One person who should have a fairly decent estimation on the size of the New Age is best-selling author Eckhart Tolle. In a recent interview, he revealed the following observations:

> Without considering the Eastern world, my estimate is that at this time about ten percent of people in North America are already awakening. That makes thirty million Americans alone, . . . about ten percent of the population of Western European countries is also awakening. This is probably sufficient *critical mass** to bring about a new earth. (emphasis mine)[2]

The Mystery Schools

M any people have a kind of bemused contempt for those involved with mysticism, and thus, they believe that the New Age movement is a frivolous frolic into the absurd.

In answer to this, I would like to emphasize two points. First, millions of people are having *real experiences.* Second, these experiences are as old as human civilization.

It is important to understand that the foundation upon which the New Age movement is based transcends the mere intellectual acceptance of ideas. It cannot be seen as separate from the mystical experience from which it springs.

The Mystery Schools are the most easily documented of the ancient adherents of occultism. They were the caretakers of this esoteric (hidden) knowledge.

These schools formed the nucleus of the religious practices of ancient nations and empires such as Egypt, China, Chaldea, Persia, Greece, and Rome, as well as the Aztec and Inca civilizations.

---

* Critical Mass - The idea that a particular belief or behavior can be accepted by all of society once a certain number of people have aligned.

The Mystery religions were so labeled because their teachings were kept hidden from the common people. In fact, the term occult (meaning hidden or concealed) originated from the Mystery religions because the majority of people were ignorant of their true meanings. Only the priests and adepts (who were initiated through various grades or levels) gained insight into these hidden *truths* of the universe.

What was kept hidden or secret? It can best be summed up as the knowledge of the *laws and forces* that underlie the universe but are not evident to the five senses of man's normal perception. Basically, they taught an awareness of the invisible worlds for wisdom and guidance and the development of psychic abilities and spiritual *healing techniques.*

New Age writers often refer to the core teachings of occultism as the *Ancient Wisdom.* They also refer to it as the *Secret Wisdom, Ageless Wisdom,* and the *Perennial Wisdom.* Many believe this Ancient Wisdom can be traced back to the fabled civilization of Atlantis.

Despite enormous geographical distances and cultural differences, *the Mysteries* all taught the same message: "Happy and blessed one, you have become divine instead of mortal."[3]

Theosophical Society

If we were to mark any particular beginning of the modern New Age movement, it would have to be the founding of the Theosophical Society. *Theos* is the Greek word for God and *sophos* is the word for wisdom. The Theosophical Society became the society for the study of *the wisdom of the Divine.*

The Society was started in 1875, in New York City by Helena Petrovna Blavatsky (a Russian noblewoman) and Col. Henry Olcott, an American occultist.

The main purpose of Theosophy, as it was called, was to open the door for occult teachings to spread throughout Western society. It concentrated on the development of *occult powers* within the individual rather than concerning itself simply with contacting the dead, as did the spiritualist movement. The following statement can best explain the core of Theosophy:

> Theosophical teachers have all repeated the old, old doctrine as the fundamental on which to build—the doctrine that the real human being is not the poor weak creature he too often thinks he is, and exhibits to others, but a wondrous *spiritual being* in the innermost recesses of his nature, a divine mystery, and that it is within his power to find himself, and indeed it is his destiny, to realize this and eventually become it.[4]

Madame Blavatsky (also known as HPB) was one of the most illustrious figures of modern occultism. She inspired thousands of people all over the world to embrace the Ancient Wisdom. The publicity that surrounded her fueled this interest to a large degree. The following story is typical of the way she would respond to those that doubted the validity of the Theosophical philosophy:

> At a party, she materialized a cup and saucer. Outraged by suggestions that she might have planted them, she asked her hostess if there was anything she particularly wanted. The hostess mentioned a brooch she had lost some years before. After communicating with her "masters," HPB announced that it was buried in a flower-bed. The company trooped outside, dug among the flowers, and promptly found the brooch.[5]

Although Theosophy's influence has greatly waned, Theosophical lodges can still be found around the world. The Theosophical Society was instrumental in beginning what is now known as the New Age movement.

Alice Ann Bailey

In the early twentieth century, a figure who would have a major impact upon the western esoteric movement came out of Theosophy. The popularization of the very name New Age has been attributed to her writings. Her name was Alice Ann Bailey.

Born Alice LaTrobe-Bateman in Manchester, England on June 16, 1880, she grew up as a society girl and enjoyed all the privileges of the British upper-class. Alice, being very religious, met and married a man who later became an Episcopal minister. In time, they moved to the United States.

When Alice's husband physically abused her, she left him and settled with her three children in Pacific Grove, California. There she met two other English women who brought her great comfort. These women introduced her to Theosophy, which seemed to provide answers to Alice's questions concerning why such misfortune had befallen her. Alice, then thirty-five, was about to have her life changed forever. Later, in her unfinished autobiography, she wrote:

> I discovered, first of all, that there is a great and divine Plan. . . . I discovered, for a second thing, that there are Those Who are responsible for the working out of that Plan and Who, step by step and stage by stage, have led mankind on down the centuries.[6]

In 1917, Alice moved to Los Angeles and began working for that plan at the Theosophical headquarters where she met Foster Bailey, a man who had devoted his life to the Ancient Wisdom. She divorced her husband and married Bailey in 1920.

Alice had her *first* contact with a voice that claimed to be a master in November of 1919. Calling himself the "Tibetan," he wanted Alice to take dictation from him. Concerning this, Alice wrote:

> I heard a voice which said, "There are some books
> which it is desired should be written for the public.
> You can write them. Will you do so?"[7]

Alice felt reluctant at first to take on such an unusual endeavor but the voice continued urging her to write the books.
Alice experienced a brief period of anxiety in which she feared
for her health and sanity. She was finally reassured by one of her
other masters that she had nothing to fear and that she would
be doing a "really valuable piece of work."[8]

The "valuable work" Alice was to do lasted thirty years. Between 1919 and 1949, by means of telepathic communication,
Alice Bailey wrote nineteen books for her unseen mentor.

To occultists, the significance of the Alice Bailey writings was
that they foretold that in the coming Aquarian Age "the teachings
of the East and of the West must be fused and blended before
the true and universal religion—for which the world waits—could
appear on earth."*[9]

There also would be a "Coming One,"[10] whom she called
"the Christ,"[11] who would not be the Lord Jesus Christ whom
Christians await the return of, but an entirely different individual. This man would embody all the great principles of occultism, chiefly the *divinity and perfectibility of man*, and consequently
expect recognition and honor as to his *own* lordship and divinity.

A Targeted Generation

Prior to the late 1960s, occultism in America was relatively
obscure and considered an eccentric pursuit. If such ideas were
discussed in public, the person expressing them would have been
considered peculiar.

The 1960s changed all that in a relatively short period of time.
I remember once having a conversation with an elderly lady who

---

* This one sentence sums up the entire theme of my book, A *Time of Departing*.

had been involved with occultism all of her life. She recounted to me how New Age thought "hadn't really gotten anywhere until the hippies came along, then things really started to get off the ground." Her observation could not have been more accurate.

Many people think of the 1960s as a time when a bunch of outlandish young people acted up and tweaked the nose of *straight* society. In reality, it was a social and cultural revolution of gigantic proportion. These shifts in attitudes during the 1960s deeply affected the social fabric of the entire Western world.

The youth/drug/rock counterculture, as it was called, could be broken down into three basic segments:

> *The Radical Political Element:* Collectively known as the *New Left,* they wanted to *off the pig* (kill police), *smash the state,* and give *power to the people.* In other words, they considered themselves to be the politically motivated vanguard who would lead progressive elements of society in a broad-based socialist revolt against what they perceived as the capitalist/imperialist coalition of government and military. In addition to those who wanted revolution, there were many who simply wanted to see the war in Vietnam end.

> *The Hedonists:* These were the ones who really just wanted to party. This meant getting stoned, engaging in promiscuous sex, listening to Jimi Hendrix or the Jefferson Airplane, looking hip, and giving lip service to whatever seemed to be fashionable at the time. They had no real commitment to anything other than their own pleasure.

> *The Spiritual Seekers:* These were the ones who had spiritual insights from their involvement with drugs (mainly LSD) and Eastern mystical practices. They were into yoga, I-Ching, tarot cards, astrology, Zen, Native American lifestyles, Atlantis, UFOs, ESP, Eastern gurus, reincarnation, holistic health, and other such interests. In other words, instead of Marxism and pleasure seeking,

these people were delving into the Ancient Wisdom as the answer to the world's problems. What made them significant is that they numbered in the *millions*.

Those in New Age circles have rallied around and taken very seriously a book called *The Starseed Transmissions*, purportedly channeled from a being who called himself "Raphael." Many highly respected New Age leaders, such as Jean Houston, have praised it for telling us what the intention and plan of the New Age is really all about. The book gives some keen insights. In it, Raphael describes the mission he and his kind are pursuing:

> There is but the flimsiest of screens between your present condition and your true nature. It is our mission to assist you in bridging this gap, to awaken you from sleep, to bring you to the fulfillment of your destiny.[12]

According to Raphael, the 1960s played a key role in this mission. This is very apparent in his comments about that time period. He speaks of their [Raphael and his fellow spiritual entities] first large scale entry into our "historical process" in the late 1960s:

> At that time, the members of your species most responsive to our descending vibrational patterns were those who had not yet assumed clearly defined social roles. Within them, we could plant the seeds of our Life-giving information with the greatest chance for successful germination.... We chose the years 1967 to 1969 for this first large scale experiment, because at that time in your global civilization there was an entire generation coming into maturity that was receptive to change on a planetary scale.[13]

What Raphael said he and his kind were going to do *has happened* just the way he explained it would. The generation that embraced these metaphysical ideas in the 1960s has been the catalyst for the current surge of spiritual transformation that is now permeating our society. Because of this, occultism is no longer a proper term for the Ancient Wisdom since it is *not* hidden from view or kept secret any more. In *fact*, just the *opposite* is now the case. Being anything *but* hidden, it is highly visible and available to anyone. I heard one practitioner on the radio put it very aptly when he said that in the last twenty years occultism has come out of the closet, and it will *never* be driven back in.

Another metaphysician made a similar concurrence by stating:

> At one time such cosmic knowledge was hard to come by. It was known as the mystery teachings, or the occult (hidden) teachings, or the secret doctrine and it was only available to selected individuals in secret retreats which have always existed on Earth. Now it is available to all who are interested.[14]

The New Age Around the World

The New Age phenomenon is by no means confined only to America. In virtually every country in the world you can find evidence that it is having an impact. In countries such as India, Japan, and Nigeria, it has been the traditional spirituality for centuries. In many others, especially countries that have been traditionally Christian, the New Age movement is expanding. Germany is a good example of this. Consider the following quotes in a West German magazine from the 1980s:

> [The movement] has exploded in the BRD (West Germany) - [since] 1986 an infrastructure has spread out. . . . it is very typical of the early phases of a mass movement. . . . Germany is over-ripe for New Age," says Gerd Gerken of the Creative House. "In this country there is a high potential for the transformation."[15]

Great Britain has also been engulfed in the New Age tide. One annual New Age festival, the Glastonbury Festival, has been in existence since 1970 and draws a crowd of 150,000 each year.[16] A sympathetic English clergyman had this to say:

> The popularity of the Meditation movement today is beyond doubt. All sections of society, religious and secular, urban and rural have felt its impact. It is everywhere apparent, from the now familiar groups meeting regularly in church halls for the practice of Yoga to the recent invasion of rural Sussex by Buddhist contemplatives.[17]

The New Age view has become so respectable and mainstream in Great Britain that some very notable personalities have no qualms about endorsing practices that are distinctly metaphysical. One popular healer in London who uses occult energies in her work has the openly public support of none other than Sarah Ferguson, the Duchess of York, widely known as *Fergie*:

> Alla [the healer] has been a tremendous help in guiding me in all aspects of my physical and emotional well being. Whenever I go to see her, she recharges my energy and enables me to cope with the many challenges and demands of my busy life. She offers me sound practical advice that I'm sure would make sense to anyone who is struggling to find time to focus on their health in the midst of a hectic lifestyle.[18]

This healer is also endorsed by Elizabeth Hurley, one of the most beautiful and high profile models and actresses in Great Britain.

Back in the Soviet Union in the 1980s, there was a thriving interest in Aquarian pursuits. A book on citizen diplomacy to the Soviet Union at the time revealed:

Growing numbers of Soviets *are* experimenting with and avidly pursuing interests in meditation, yoga, vegetarianism, exercise, massage, encounter groups, gestalt groups, *est*, underwater birthings, crystals, psychic healing, clairvoyance, telepathy, Aikido and transformationalism... Literature on yoga, sufism, Buddhism, Vedanta, Cabala, the lost knowledge of ancient civilizations, and other esoteric subjects is available and finds a wide audience.. .we know for certain that many top officials are involved in these activities themselves.[19]

Today, Russian metaphysical pursuits are still going strong, very strong! In her fascinating book on modern Russia, *Moscow Days*, journalist Galina Dutkina explains:

[T]here have never been so many people involved with the occult sciences and paranormal phenomena in Russia as there are now. Two years ago the evidence of this was only bubbling on the surface like foam, but now it has penetrated throughout everyday life. Wherever you look on television or in the newspapers, astrologists and magicians, shamans and traditional psychics, warlocks and witches, healers and medicine men, seers and clairvoyants, . . . There are numerous schools, courses, and academies of all types where you can learn these crafts yourself, where there are courses in telling fortunes by the stars, healing, casting spells, and harnessing or simply invoking the forces of darkness or cosmic energy.[20]

This New Age was getting so formidable in China it actually threatened the government and communist party. In 1999, the Chinese government banned the mystical sect called "Falun Gong" or "Falun Dafa" in order to keep it from seriously challenging the status quo. Falun Gong "incorporates Buddhist and Taoist principles"[21] using meditation exercises to deepen spiritual awareness. Apparently this appealed to a great many spiritually hungry Chinese. The group claimed 100 million followers at the time of the crackdown.

Religion or Science?

In the last twenty years, many groups and individuals have come forward with various *psycho-technologies* for maximizing *personal growth* and *human potential*—this potential being in the higher self. New Agers understand that metaphysics must be presented in a way which will attract the greatest number of people—the advantage being that those who might reject any perceived attempts to slip them religion of any kind, would find the idea of growth techniques acceptable. Maharishi Mahesh Yogi did this with his Transcendental Meditation program emphasizing "the Science of Creative Intelligence" rather than mantra yoga, which is what it really is. Others have promoted scientific sounding terms like *alpha state awareness* or *intuition development*, which are just imaginative names for meditation.

The advantage New Agers have in enacting significant change in our society is evident in the following quote:

> Metaphysics can be taught in highly religious terms, or it can be taught as a pure science, without any religious connotations whatsoever.[22]

When metaphysics is presented as a science, it is possible for a person to not be aware of its spiritual influence. Many people now coming into direct contact with the Ancient Wisdom do not realize nor understand what it's all about. They may be told it concerns the latest findings on *human development*, since many times the people presenting it do not want them to know its true nature. The goal is to merge these practices into society so they will be considered normal and acceptable. To accomplish this, they change terms; meditation becomes *centering*, and the higher self may be called anything that sounds positive. The key is to rename any terminology that might turn people off. A metaphysics teacher once boasted to me that, "All I have to do is drop the mystical connotations and businessmen eat this stuff up. *The experience sells itself.*"

The following example illustrates this point well: I was talking once with the owner of a New Age bookstore when I noticed she had the hard-core *material* (i.e., channeling, spirit guides, etc.) located toward the back of the store, while the more mainstream books (i.e., self-help, holistic health, transpersonal psychology, etc.) were up in front. I made the comment that no difference between the two existed since they were both based on opening yourself up to the power of the higher self. The owner's face broke into an impish grin and, putting her index finger over her lips in a hush gesture, she replied, "I know, but don't tell anybody."

A Subtle Effort

I knew of another store in a major West Coast city that sold books, tapes, and videos on stress reduction. An entire room was devoted to posting fliers and brochures on metaphysical workshops and seminars in the area.

The owners were very active in their community. Doctors, therapists, and teachers came to them for help. They have given talks to school faculties, major corporations, all the major hospitals in their city, churches, service organizations, and senior citizen groups. Their clientele tended to be affluent, well-educated professionals and business people who are interested in *personal growth*.

They emphasized such seemingly beneficial endeavors as stress reduction and self-improvement with an additional element added—*spiritual awareness*. One of them related how she attended a powerful workshop with "Lazaris" and discovered his techniques were practical and usable. That doesn't sound too extraordinary until you find out Lazaris is not a person but a *spirit guide*. Considering the possible nature of that workshop, listen to what a brochure on Lazaris had to say:

> There will be several incredible Guided Meditations and the very touching Blendings with Lazaris. A Blending is when Lazaris combines his energy with ours to touch us individually either to impart knowledge into our Subconscious or to help us create the reality we desire. The Blendings are very intimate times to just be with Lazaris.[23]

Because of our stereotypes of people who previously gravitated toward mystical experiences (such as counterculture types), we may tend to assume that people associated with the New Age movement are odd-looking, have strange personalities, or are in other ways offbeat. The two owners I have just described are very bright, articulate, well-dressed, and above all, *extremely personable*.

A newspaper reporter who did an article on one of them informed me that she was "one of the most calm, serene persons I have ever met." The reporter added, "*People want what she has.*"

I wonder what she would have said had she known this serenity was probably the result of *blendings* with a spirit guide and that this woman was promoting the same state-of-being to others on a wide scale.

Missions to Accomplish

Those involved in the New Age movement do not work by accident or coincidence. Rather, they have a mission to accomplish and receive inner guidance to show them where, when, and how that work must be done.

A woman I am acquainted with told me about a situation that happened to her. One evening a stranger began chatting with her. She had never met him, yet he told her things about her early life that he had *no possible way of knowing*. The accuracy of his information about her past greatly disturbed her. The man then explained why he had approached her. He said he had been "sent to save" her and that he was guided to her by a "central source of wisdom," and told her that she, too, could get in touch with that *same source*. He promised her that once she had connected with it she could have anything she wanted in life. Greatly unnerved, she quickly departed from his company.

New Age writer David Spangler makes it clear who or what this "central source of wisdom" is and what it wants to accomplish. Referring to his own spirit guide, "John," he writes:

> Over the years it has been evident that John's main interest is the emergence of a new age and a new culture, and he identifies himself as one of those on the spiritual side of life whose work is specifically to empower that emergence.[24]

We must conclude then that the New Age movement does not have any real leaders, only followers. I heard one writer/channeler put it very plainly when he revealed:

> Everyone anywhere who tunes into the Higher Self becomes part of the transformation. Their lives then become orchestrated from other realms.[25]

This aspect *must* be understood in order to fully grasp the significance of the New Age movement.

It may appear on the surface that all of these groups and individuals are not connected, but the following quote sheds light on the real situation. One New Age writer confirmed:

> Soon it also became apparent that those of us experiencing this inner contact were instinctively (and spontaneously) drawing together, forming a network. In the many years since, I have watched

this network grow and widen to literally encompass the globe. What was once a rare experience—that of meeting another person who admitted to a similar superconscious presence in his or her life—has now become a common, even frequent, event . . . what I once saw as a personal (and individual) transformation I now see as part of a *massive and collective human movement* (emphasis mine).[26]

In his extremely revealing and insightful 1980s book, *The Emerging New Age*, sociologist J. L. Simmons disclosed that "tens of thousands" of metaphysical teachers and counselors existed in America who were in the process of training and guiding "hundreds of thousands" of students and clients. In addition to these, "millions" had "a sporadic but real interest" in metaphysics. Simmons observed:

Each of these circles is growing in numbers. And there is a steady progression of people inward: an uncommitted person moves into the active, part-time circle, and so on.[27]

Simmons concluded that because of this swell of interest the movement was "doubling in size every three to five years."[28] The Ancient Wisdom wasn't just for cave-dwelling mystics anymore! This prediction has been backed up by some very respectable and knowledgeable scholars. One is Professor James Herrick, who wrote an in-depth book on this subject. From Herrick's astute vantage point there has been an:

. . . enormous effort to replace society's spiritual base with a wholly new one . . . [that by] dismantling the old view . . . and fashioning a new and presumably better one in its place.[29]

This process of dismantling the old and fashioning the new is what *For Many Shall Come In My Name* is all about. As Professor Herrick points out in his book, this shift is not mere speculation, it is a fact!

An October 2006 *Time* magazine article on what America believes, reveals that fourteen percent of the U.S. population sees God as "a Higher Power or Cosmic Force."[30] This would confirm the number that Eckhart Tolle spoke of (thirty million New Agers). How would any movement achieve such an enormous following so quickly? What is it that drives such rapid growth? The answer to this question cannot be ignored or dismissed as irrelevant.

THREE

ON THE PATH

THE New Age movement is very diverse and offers a broad array of *spiritual paths* that promise enlightenment and wholeness. Anyone seeking to expand his or her consciousness has varying options for satisfying this desire. By examining and understanding the various New Age paths, a person discovers a method suited to every taste and personality, from the most outrageous to the most respectable and seemingly scientific.

By far, there are more women involved with the New Age than men, as women are generally more interested in spiritual things. New Agers tend to be white, affluent, well-educated, and achievement-oriented with a general bent toward idealism and service to others. Most are concerned about world peace, ecology, and positive social action. This idealism is consistent with occult philosophy, for one of Alice Bailey's primary goals in bringing in the New Age was to achieve "right human relations."[1]

How Large?

So, how large *is* the New Age movement? In his fascinating book on the subject, *Spiritual But Not Religious*, Professor Robert C. Fuller of Bradley University answered this question by asserting "a full 20 percent of the population can be said to be sympathetic with the New Age movement."[2] This would be somewhere around forty million people over the age of 21. This figure ties in with estimates of researchers at the University of California who believed forty million persons were either involved or open to involvement in the 1990s. If this number sounds inflated, I would encourage skeptics to just count the shelves devoted to metaphysics or Eastern mysticism at any large chain bookstore where there are anywhere from sixty to eighty shelves covering this theme. Going by the law of the market, Professor Fuller's numbers appear to be an accurate estimation.

The New Age movement can be broken down into the following elements: New Thought, Eastern religion, Wicca/shamanic, human potential, metaphysical schools, and social/political activism. The following is a brief synopsis of each—

New Thought

One of the most conventional and acceptable elements of the New Age is New Thought. The terms are used interchangeably in many books and articles. New Thought is basic metaphysics refined and made palatable for the person who might find these teachings unacceptable in their original format. For this reason, New Thought attracts a very mainstream and respectable following.

New Thought has wide appeal because it places great emphasis on being positive and excludes anything that even smacks of negativity. Since those of New Thought persuasions believe reality is created by a person's thoughts, it's important for them to try to dwell only on positive thoughts.

Religious groups such as *Unity School of Christianity* (commonly known as *Unity*), *United Church of Religious Science* and *Religious Science International* (both known as *Science of Mind*), *Church of Divine Science*, and numerous independent churches adhere to the principles of New Thought. New Thought has had a substantial impact on American religion that is still growing and extends far beyond the number of New Thought churches and their regular members. One religious news writer reports about the influence of New Thought in America:

> Prof. Ferenc M. Szasz of the University of New Mexico, author of several books on American religions, says that New Thought has become the "primary faith" of millions of Americans and the "auxiliary faith" of millions more.[3]

This growth has been accomplished primarily through the explosion of self-help books written by New Thought authors such as Eric Butterworth, Catherine Ponder, Joel Goldsmith, Joseph Murphy, and Louise Hay (who has become popular with her best seller *You Can Heal Your Life.*)

New Thought fits the category of New Age because it embraces the traditional occult doctrine that *all* human beings are manifestations of God, that there is only one power in the universe (God), and that man is a part of that power. Practitioners believe that this power is the divine inner essence of man, and when a person taps into that power and understands the *truth* about himself, he may create for himself unlimited prosperity and happiness.

Despite New Thought's extensive use of Christian terminology—concepts such as the fall of man, sin, the virgin birth, salvation by faith, redemption by Christ's blood, and the final judgment of all men (the main tenets of Christianity)—all are completely rejected by New Thought as false and irrational. New

Thought teaches that sin is ignorance of divine law and that heaven and hell are states of consciousness rather than actual places. Jesus Christ is considered to be a great example of what we all can become—a man who manifested his own *Christ Self* or higher self to the fullest.

Even though New Thought presents itself as being conventional and approved of, the basic belief structure behind it is the same as Theosophy. In reality, New Thought could be called Theosophy with a "Christian" veneer. One New Age writer acknowledged this by stating:

> Many people are theosophists without being members of the Theosophical Society. Most people that are interested in new thought, the oneness of humanity, and spiritual evolution could consider themselves theosophists.[4]

Even though many people have little or no awareness of New Thought as a spiritual movement, two of the most influential religious leaders of the last fifty years have strong New Thought connections. The first one, Norman Vincent Peale, said of Unity World headquarters, called Unity Village:

> I have been spiritually fed by this place for many years. I am personally glad to acknowledge the debt of gratitude that I owe to Unity for many spiritual insights and growth, and for the help that it has given me in my ministry over the years.[5]

Peale said he believed the movement was "good" because it "has brought the Divine into the consciousness of untold thousands of people."[6] Religious author Charles Braden saw Peale as one of New Thought's major advocates. He explains:

> The man through whose ministry essentially New Thought ideas and techniques have been made

known most widely in America is Norman Vincent
Peale . . . He is reaching more people than any other
single minister in America and perhaps the world.[7]

One of those whom he reached became even more influential than he was. That person is Robert Schuller, widely known
for his many books on the power of possibility thinking, his
television show *Hour of Power*, and his church the Crystal Cathe-
dral. But what many might not know about Schuller is his New
Thought proclivities. Interspiritual scholar Marcus Bach once
related the following incident that took place at a Unity church
in Hawaii in which Bach was speaking:

> Dr. Schuller attended the first of three services, this
> one at 7:30 am. When we shook hands at the door,
> he tarried to assure me how much Unity principles
> meant to him and how helpful they had been to
> him in his work.[8]

What could some of these Unity principles be? Bach explains:

> Hinduism's emphasis on meditation fit[s] well into
> Unity's patterns for enlightenment.[9]

This is one of the major principles that Schuller was making
reference to. In his own book, *Prayer: My Soul's Adventure with
God*, he says:

> Move into mighty moods of meditation. Draw
> energy from centers of sacred solitude, serenity,
> and silence. . . . Find yourself coming alive in the
> garden of prayer called *meditation*. . . . Yes, the "New
> Agers" have grabbed hold of meditation. . . . Hey,
> Christian! Hear me! Let's not give up the glorious,
> God-given gift of meditation by turning it over to
> those outside our faith.[10]

The point that Schuller misses is that meditation is what makes a person a New Ager! This perspective is something to consider in light of the quarter million pastors who have trained and been mentored under Schuller at his Leadership Institute.

Eastern Religion

It used to be common practice by both the secular press and evangelical Christianity to refer to the New Age movement as simply *Eastern mysticism*. This may have been more accurate during the 1960s and 1970s, and although still true to a certain degree, it is only part of the whole picture.

During the counterculture period, many *gurus* (spiritual teachers) came to the West to spread the Ancient Wisdom, Hindu and Buddhist style, to a generation of young people who had, in many cases, rejected the religious traditions of their parents. This period could be accurately labeled *the era of the guru*. The traditions that made up this Eastern wave included *Hinduism* (India), *Sikhism* (India), *Zen Buddhism* (Japan), *Tantric Buddhism* (Tibet), and *Sufism* (Islam).

Various yogis (masters of yoga techniques), swamis (members of Hindu religious orders), and Babas (spiritual fathers) came to America, established ashrams (spiritual centers) and acquired followings of chelas (pupils who sit at the feet of a guru). They would engage in satsang (spiritual lecture by a guru) and dharmah (spiritually harmonious living). Some groups, such as the Hare Krishnas and Sikhs, would adopt Indian dress and customs, but the vast majority of devotees retained their western cultural veneer and changed only their mindset.

Traditional ethnic Hinduism would not have easily implanted on North American soil because of the wide cultural differences. Instead, Eastern thought has evolved into the broader New Age movement, which is better suited for western cultural tastes. The Indian gurus have spawned huge numbers of *American gurus* who, although they may lack the exotic look of their

Indian mentors, are just as committed to spreading the Ancient Wisdom as their masters were.

A perfect example of just how widespread Eastern religion has become in our Western world is the popular practice of yoga. In the beginning of the 21st century, around twenty million Americans are doing this practice based on Eastern religion, often in church recreation halls and at the YMCA.[11]

Wicca

One day I was having a conversation with a waitress I knew. She told me she had dressed her little girl in a witch costume for a Halloween party. The young mother told me how cute her little girl looked. She added, "Of course, I told my daughter there are no real witches." When she said that, I thought, *if you only knew.* Most people think of witches in relation to elves, fairies, and goblins—something out of children's Halloween stories or the Wizard of Oz. The truth is, witchcraft has become a major religious movement, especially among women. And as with all New Age sub-groups, meditative practices play an integral part in Wicca. One Wiccan writer acknowledged, "Solitary meditation and visualization practice are part of every Witch's training."[12] Wicca accepts the doctrines of reincarnation and karma and strongly identifies with the belief that mankind is entering the Age of Aquarius.

Modern witches strongly deny any charge that they are connected with Satan or the Devil. They insist that the belief in Satan is a Christian concept, and since they are not Christian, they cannot worship a being they do not believe exists. They believe that man is basically good and that there is no *evil being* to lead people astray. Wicca, in this respect, is very similar to New Thought. What Wiccans (or witches) claim to worship are the *forces of nature* as personified by various gods and goddesses. Because there are goddesses in Wicca, many women have embraced the movement and elevated the goddess over any male deity. This has been called the *Woman Spirit movement,* a combination of feminism and witchcraft that has greatly contributed to the recent surge of interest in Wicca.

I was able to obtain a copy of a catalog from a publishing house that caters predominately to a Wiccan clientele. The catalog held a wide variety of titles on such topics as doing spells, reading tarot cards, astral travel, past lives and such. What struck me most was the massive popularity of these subjects. Featured in the front of the catalog were the company's top 36 best-selling titles. All totaled, these titles had sold over *seven* million copies within a relatively short time span. In addition, the catalog featured over 500 titles, virtually all of them on Wiccan themes and practices. One author alone, Silver Ravenwolf (her witch name) has sold over a million copies of her books, with the most popular titles being: *To Ride a Silver Broomstick* (over 300,000 copies sold); *The Solitary Witch* (200,000 sold); and the immensely influential *Teen Witch* (200,000 sold).[13]

Shamanism, or tribal folk magic, is an area related to witchcraft which has grown tremendously in recent years. This can be seen by the popularity of books by authors such as Carlos Castaneda and Michael Harner. Also related is the Afro-Latin American spiritist religion of Santeria, whose devotees rival the numbers of Wicca. There are reported to be hundreds of thousands of believers among American urban populations of Cubans and Puerto Ricans.

Human Potential

The human potential movement sprang out of the *growth center* phenomenon of the 1960s and 1970s. First started by the Esalen Institute of Big Sur, California, it has spread extensively throughout American society. Many groups and individuals have come forward with various *psycho-technologies* for maximizing *personal growth* and *human potential*—this potential being the higher self. The human potential movement understands metaphysics must be presented in a way that will attract the greatest number of people—the advantage being that people, who might reject any perceived attempts to slip them religion of any kind, would find the idea of *growth techniques* acceptable in their desire to improve their lives.

Stripped of religious connotations, many groups and individuals offer their training to a wide variety of both public and private institutions, businesses, schools, medical/health centers, city, state, and federal government agencies who are eagerly exploring these possibilities. Even the U.S. military is involved. A book on the post-Vietnam army reveals:

> Eighty of our best generals have already been trained
> in the most advanced consciousness principles of
> the New Age.[14]

A good example is the Landmark Forum (previously known as *est* or Erhard Seminar Training), which in the 70s and 80s trained hundreds of thousands of professionals in human potential modalities. Today, the Landmark Forum seminar is still going strong with over 160,000 participants each year on six continents.[15] That could mean around two and half million people have been influenced since the early 90s.

Another popular human potential venue is the Silva Method formerly known as Silva Mind Control. The Silva Method has been around for over forty years and is taught by Certified Silva Method Instructors (CSMIs). According to the Silva Method website, over four million people worldwide have been taught this method of human potentiality from 111 countries in thirty languages.[16]

Therapeutic

Probably the most dynamic element that has caused the New Age to explode in popularity is the therapeutic appeal. Many people have no qualms about trying meditation for health or well-being reasons. There are other modes called *energy healing* that are also gaining in popularity.

A good example of this is the popularity of yoga. Millions of people, mainly women, have turned to yoga for health-enhancement reasons. Many believe yoga is merely stretching exercises to keep one fit. But the word yoga actually translates as *union* as in joining together. What you are united with is the higher self or Atman (the Hindu word for higher self). This is called self-realization. That is why at the beginning of every yoga class the teacher says to the students Namaste' (the god in me bows down to the god in you).

Energy healing is another New Age modality that is gaining momentum. What this entails is a force or energy pouring out of the practitioner's hands into the client or subject. This energy always has a spiritual component and is supposed to alleviate a variety of ills and problems. Names that apply to this method includes Reiki, therapeutic touch, healing touch, quantum touch, Pranic healing, and Brennan Healing Science.

This appeal to health has such a draw that I have devoted two entire chapters to this theme.

Metaphysical Schools

Until the 1960s occult explosion, the major focus of metaphysical endeavor in America was the esoteric schools. These organizations are in many ways the modern counterparts of the ancient Mystery Schools, and many consider themselves heirs and caretakers of the Ancient Wisdom. They tend to emphasize metaphysics as a philosophy of life and consider dispensing higher consciousness a sacred task that should only be offered to the noble of heart and the serious of mind.

Groups that would fit this description are the *Theosophical Society, Arcane School, Association For Research and Enlightenment,* and *Rosicrucians* (AMORC), and an array of lesser schools, brotherhoods, lodges, and societies.

Although metaphysics has greatly expanded and become more mainstream and diverse, these groups still play an important role in anchoring the Ancient Wisdom. Whereas New Thought and human potential groups advocate metaphysical development as a means to achieve prosperity and personal happiness, many esoteric societies stress spiritual awareness as a prerequisite for *service to humanity*. Idealism is a very prevalent element in their world vision.

Many of these groups have produced courses that have been successful in offering metaphysics to the public at large. One such organization is the Berkeley Psychic Institute, which was started by former Rosicrucian Lewis S. Bostwick. Around 100,000 people have taken meditation classes through the Institute and thousands have graduated with the authority to teach people psychic abilities.[17] The Institute also puts out a monthly newspaper called *Psychic Reader* with a circulation of 139,000.[18]

One relatively new school, Wisdom University, boasts a who's who of the New Age for their faculty: Dr. Lauren Artress, who has had a major influence on bringing the labyrinth, an ancient meditative tool, to mainstream society; Andrew Harvey, a homosexual mystic who wrote *The Essential Gay Mystic*; psychic Jean Houston; and Barbara Marx Hubbard, president of the Foundation for Conscious Evolution are just a few of the university's teachers. The university "blends immersion in sacred practices [meditation] with hands-on social activism."[19]

Social/Political Activism

Although this element may not be overtly New Age in nature, it has served as a magnet for bringing together transformed New Agers and the socially concerned. Like the human potential movement, this segment grew out of the tumult of the 1960s when various *civil rights* movements sprang up from the counterculture. Never before had so many people demonstrated concern over such issues as the environment or the treatment of various minority groups.

In the 1970s and 1980s, many who had sought purely political means for world betterment in the 1960s became disillusioned with that route and endeavored to link planetary betterment with spiritual transformation. They saw simple protest was not accomplishing their goal. They were convinced that in order to *perfect the world,* they had to *perfect the people* first. Getting in tune with one's *inner divinity* was seen as the key to effecting that change on a wide scale. Meditation also seemed like an easier commitment than marches and resistance. They believed that any effort to save the world and end social evil would fail without the element of higher consciousness.

It would surprise many Americans to know that they actually voted for a New Age sympathizer for president of the United States in the 2000 election. In a *Time* magazine article in 2003 called "Just Say Om," former presidential candidate, Al Gore, said the following about meditation:

> We both [he and his wife] believe in regular prayer, and we often pray together. But meditation—as distinguished from prayer—I highly recommend it.[20]

One might argue that perhaps Gore was not referring to mystical type meditation and that he didn't have any such proclivities, but this notion would be put to rest by his endorsement of a book (*Marriage of Sense and Soul*) by Ken Wilber, a leading figure in the New Age. On the back cover of the book, Gore proudly proclaimed Wilber's book is "one of my new favorites."[21] New Ager Neale Donald Walsch publicly revealed Gore's spiritual sympathies in the following comments he made at the Humanity's Team Leadership Gathering in 2003:

> You know Al Gore. I know Al well and he says to me, "Hey Neale, I used to be the next president of the United States." Al has read my books and *loves them,* but he can't possibly say that publicly. . . . He should be able

to, and in the society we're going to recreate he will
be able to, but right now he can't. (emphasis mine)[22]

For those not familiar with Walsch's work, this may not seem
that significant. But Walsch is the author of the *Conversations
with God* books, in which millions of copies have been sold.
His books are the supposed conversations between Walsch and
"God." Walsch's "God" proclaims:

> The twenty-first century will be the time of
> awakening, of meeting The Creator Within. Many
> beings will experience Oneness with God. . . . There
> are many such people in the world now—teachers
> and messengers, Masters and visionaries—who are
> placing this vision before humankind and offering
> tools with which to create it. These messengers and
> visionaries are the heralds of a New Age.[23]

> There is only one message that can change the
> course of human history forever, end the torture,
> and bring you back to God. That message is The
> New Gospel: WE ARE ALL ONE.[24]

The "tools" Walsch is speaking of is meditation. The fact
that someone who promotes and practices New Age meditation
could have (and still may) become the president of United States,
shows clearly that this mindset plays an integral role in today's
world. This assessment can be backed up by New Age teacher
Marianne Williamson. Williamson became popular, largely
through the Oprah show. Williamson wrote a book, *A Return
to Love*, (based on the channeled New Age classic *A Course in
Miracles*). When Oprah brought Williamson onto her show—the
book became an overnight success.

A *Course in Miracles* could be referred to as the New Ager's
bible. One former New Ager explains Williamson's interest in
the political field:

Over the past decade, Williamson has continued
to champion *A Course in Miracles* in the media and
in her public appearances around the country.
A more recent book, *Healing the Soul of America*,
has enabled Williamson and the *Course* to make a
subtle transition into the political arena. Hoping
to inspire a "new gospel" approach to national and
world problems, Williamson, along with bestselling
Conversations with God author Neale Donald Walsch,
cofounded The Global Renaissance Alliance.[25]

When we comprehend Williamson's propensity towards
the New Age and meditation (as a vehicle for world peace),
it is astounding to know that Williamson is working closely
with Walter Cronkite, a former CBS news anchor and public
icon, once referred to as "the most trusted man in America."[26]
Williamson and Cronkite, along with Congressman Dennis
Kucinich, are trying to convince the US government to start a
cabinet-level Department of Peace within the executive branch
via House bill HR808. The fact that someone as mainstream as
Walter Cronkite would align himself with the openly metaphysical Williamson bespeaks of the current spiritual climate of our
society. Incidentally, the campaign to start the Department of
Peace is gaining momentum and currently has the support of
over 60 U.S. Representatives and Senators and has local grassroot
chapters in over 200 congressional districts.[27]

Williamson embodies, as few others do, the marriage between political/social idealism and the embracing of metaphysical perception. As the tone of modern spirituality changes so will
the various institutions that comprise society. In the following
chapters you will see just how this is unfolding and becoming
a reality. I believe many people are indifferent to the New Age
movement because they don't understand how it may influence
a number of areas in their everyday lives. But as you will read in
the following chapters, the Western world is encountering the
Aquarian dimension as a dynamic reality.

Four

The New Age in Business

IF there was one single group to whom the promise of creating one's own reality would have specific appeal, it would be business people. The competition in the corporate world is so keen that anything, no matter how unusual, may be eagerly embraced if it offers results. As they say in the business world, the *bottom line* is success.

The way New Age thought has crept into corporations is simple to understand. Management trainers and human resource developers hold positions where they can incorporate metaphysics into business under titles such as *Intuition Development, Right Brain Creativity,* and *Superlearning.* The New Age nature of these seminars may be introduced by employers either intentionally or unwittingly. The New Age Journal states:

> An unconventional new breed of consultant has surfaced on the corporate lecture circuit. They speak of meditation, energy flow and tapping into the unused potential of the mind. What's

more, they are spreading their Arcane curriculum
not only among the alternative entrepreneurs who
populate the capitalist fringe, but within the heart
of corporate America as well. General Electric,
IBM, Shell, Polaroid, and the Chase Manhattan
Bank are sending their fast-trackers to crash courses
in, strange as it may sound, intuition.[1]

Once, while attending a New Age convention, I was told
by one of these new breeds that resistance to New Age concepts in business was being replaced by a *new openness*. "How
you focus it is all important," he began, and then added:

> If you barge in with occult lingo it turns them off
> right away. You have to tell them how you can make
> their employees happier and get more productivity
> out of them—then they will listen. You are *really*
> teaching metaphysics, but you present it as human
> development.

The Quiet Revolution

This approach has tremendous appeal because companies
naturally want to get the most out of their people. New Agers
know this approach works to their advantage. One trainer defines
her role the following way:

> There is something new in the fact that businesses
> are taking an active interest in the potential of these
> techniques to bring about transformational change
> within large groups of people for organizational
> ends. You have to deal with the whole person—body,
> mind and spirit—if real change is to happen.[2]

In one interview, New Age writer Marilyn Ferguson echoes
the same theme:

> Business leaders have, by and large, exhausted
> *materialistic* values and are often open to *spiritual*
> values... What's more, top-level business people
> are not afraid of the transformative process,
> and typically, after I speak to them, they say, "I
> didn't know that such things were possible. I
> don't understand everything you're saying, but
> I'm going to find out about it." Whereas most
> people who don't understand new concepts
> automatically reject them, business people, who
> by nature are trained in risk taking, go after
> them.[3]

Dennis T. Jaffe, Ph.D., founder and director of the
Learning for Health Clinic in Los Angeles, had this to say:

> Many progressive companies are incorporating
> some of the inner-directed exercises I mentioned
> [in meditation and visualization] into their
> "manual of procedures" . . . These changes point to
> a quiet, inner-directed revolution that is reshaping
> many companies into being *agents of self-realization.*
> . . . *Many* social thinkers, such as Marilyn Ferguson,
> believe that because of its openness to change,
> business has the greatest potential for spiritualizing
> the world. (emphasis mine)[4]

A number of courses, books, and individuals are having a great
impact on the business world. Michael Ray and Rochelle Myers
have written a book titled *Creativity in Business.* The book is based
on a Stanford University course that they claim has "revolution-
ized the art of success."[5] Two people who enthusiastically endorse
this book are Spencer Johnson, MD., coauthor of *The One Minute
Manager,* and Tom Peters, coauthor of *In Search of Excellence.* Sili-
con Valley Bank Chairman, N.W. Medearis, says the book is "an
experience which will leave one significantly changed."[6]

Ray and Myers acknowledge that the book takes much of its inspiration from "Eastern philosophies, mysticism, and meditation techniques" and that "dozens of America's brightest and most successful business practitioners and entrepreneurs have contributed to the course and to this book."[7]

It is absolutely amazing how unabashed *Creativity in Business* is in recommending its source of creativity. In one section we find the heading, "Getting in Touch with Your Inner Guide." It reads:

> In this exercise you meet your wisdom-keeper or spirit guide—an inner person who can be with you in life, someone to whom you can turn for guidance.[8]

These beings are contacted either through meditative breathing exercises or with mantra meditation. If there is any doubt the book is talking about New Age meditation, it is resolved upon reading:

> As meditation master Swami Muktananda says: "We do not meditate just to relax a little and experience some peace. We meditate to unfold our inner being."[9]

Tarot cards are even presented as a source of creativity. As with other New Age categories, it begins with breathing exercises (or as the book says, *go into silence*). The person then picks the cards, which are supposed to give "some important insights."[10]

A new generation of New Age business gurus is starting to emerge on the scene. One of the more prominent is T. Harv Eker, who leads "Millionaire Mind Seminars" through his company Peak Potentials Training. This is one of the fastest growing corporate training companies in the country today, with 250,000 trainees to date. What these eager folks learn is apparent by Eker's statement that his "Mission is to educate and inspire people to live in their Higher Self."[11]

This is a typical approach. You will recall an earlier quote, "businessmen eat this stuff up, the experience sells itself." That is why it is making such headway, it works. If these methods work for people in business today the way they worked for Madame Blavatsky in finding the woman's lost brooch related in chapter two, then it's easy to see the implications of metaphysics in the business world.

Quite often I will hear people from a certain age group and social outlook dismiss what I am researching with terms such as "weirdo hippie religion." When I hear this, I think of articles appearing in such well respected magazines as *U.S. News & World Report* which paint a far different picture. One article in particular dealt specifically with New Age spirituality in the corporate world. It was called "Shush. The Guy in the Cubicle is Meditating." The article disclosed that such consultants had become "the darlings of business circles"[12] and not just *any* business circles:

> [W]hen 2,000 global powerbrokers gathered for the elite World Economic Forum in Davos, Switzerland, the agenda included confabs on "spiritual anchors for the new millennium" and "the future of meditation in a networked economy." Indeed, 30 MBA programs now offer courses on the issue. It's also the focus of the . . . *Harvard Business School Bulletin.* (emphasis mine)[13]

What this shows is that the dismissal of New Age spirituality as hippy/dippy is very much outdated and unsound. As one corporate trainer proudly proclaimed, "What's new is that it's just entered the mainstream."

Corporate "Wellness"

Creativity is not the only New Age avenue into the corporate scene. Health and fitness programs presented in the context of *corporate wellness* are becoming increasingly popular. Executives give a willing ear to ways of keeping productivity up and absenteeism down.

Many of these programs have metaphysical motives within them. One such *wellness expert* promoting *total health* explained how she was able to teach mantra meditation to a group of businessmen:

> Just yesterday I met with a whole room of executives for breakfast—top executives in a huge multinational company. . . . Here were these executives closing their eyes and breathing deeply into their abdomens, and quieting their mind by repeating just one word—"relax, relax."[14]

Earlier in the interview this woman related how she had "studied metaphysics" and "meditated three or four times a day for direction."[15]

In her joy at being able to subtly introduce meditation to those who would have rejected it as being too "far out" otherwise, she commented: "Ten years ago in an American company I would have been thrown out in the street, I'm sure."[16]

Business—The Most Logical Candidate

The New Age effort to transform business is *very real* and becoming more *successful* all the time. When asked in an interview about where he thought the vanguard of transformation was in the country today, New Ager James Fadiman replied:

> What's fascinating to me is that when I met recently with some of the old-timers in the movement, I discovered that all of us had expanded from

working in growth centers to working in American business. What the business community needs, wants, and appreciates at this time are insights from the human potential movement. . . . I'm finding executives who, twenty years ago, considered the human potential movement a kind of joke and who are now recruiting specialists into the most conservative industries.[17]

Larry Wilson, coauthor of *The One Minute Sales Person*, clearly stated in an interview that metaphysics is the core of what is being taught:

The heart of our new management training represents a return to the *ancient spiritual wisdom about the true identity and power of the individual.* In our courses, we aim to empower people so they can get in touch with their creative Source and then apply the potential to every part of their lives, including their work life. (emphasis mine)[18]

Wilson also revealed in the interview that it is the higher self that is at the heart of this "ancient spiritual wisdom." He explained:

Once a sufficient number of employees get in touch with their true potential, the organization changes . . . it helps to have top management in tune with it.[19]

In another interview, the late futurist and New Age leader Willis Harman acknowledged that:

Some of the most creative and successful people in business are really part of this new paradigm movement. You can find this sort of talk going on in business. In fact, a group of business executives and myself got together and created something we call the World Business Academy, which is a network of business executives who have already gone through their own personal transformations to a considerable extent and are asking: "What's the new role of business? What's the new corporation?"[20]

International Management magazine revealed that many of the major European corporations are also eagerly embracing New Age spirituality. Included in the list were the Bank of England and the UK's Ministry of Defense and Cabinet Office.[21]

The previously mentioned individuals, and numerous others like them, are working diligently within the corporate world to bring about a paradigm shift of potentially staggering proportions. Larry Wilson acknowledged this by saying, "This new approach is changing the corporation, and that change *will* affect other institutions of our Society."[22]

This is not an understatement. In the *2007 Shift Report: Evidence of a World Transforming* by the Institute of Noetic Sciences (a New Age think tank), it reveals:

> Since 1994 more than 100,000 executives from 56 countries have taken the Self-Management and Leadership Course (SML). SML is a two-day residential retreat inspired by the principles of *raja yoga*, which advocates inner stillness through breathwork, movement, meditation, and self-inquiry as a path to wisdom and inner balance.[23]

New Agers know that if they can transform business, *they will have transformed the world.* The reason for this is that business and government feed into each other, so to speak. Many politicians are also business people, or lawyers with strong ties to business. Also, many politicians go back into the corporate world when they leave office. The two cultures are profoundly intertwined. If the corporate world goes New Age (as we see it doing) the world of government isn't far behind.

FIVE

NEW AGE IN EDUCATION

THE field of education presents an ideal setting for transformation. In virtually every area of education and instruction, from kindergarten to universities, from weekend workshops to family counseling sessions, the Ancient Wisdom is being taught either up front or covertly. This is largely happening because teachers, principals, and other administrators in particular have become involved in metaphysics. Marilyn Ferguson acknowledges:

> Of the Aquarian Conspirators surveyed, more were involved in education than in any other single category of work.[1]

These people, according to Ferguson, had already begun to attempt significant changes in the educational system. She states:

> Subtle forces are at work, factors you are not likely to see in banner headlines. For example, tens of thousands of classroom teachers, educational consultants and psychologists, counselors,

administrators, researchers, and faculty members in colleges of education have been among the millions engaged in *personal transformations*. They have only recently begun to link regionally and nationally, to share strategies, to conspire for the teaching of all they most value: freedom, high expectations, awareness, patterns, connections, creativity. They are eager to share their discoveries with those colleagues ready to listen.[2]

New Age education consists of *developing* the whole person—body, mind, and spirit—with an emphasis on the spirit. Often this is termed as *holistic* or *transpersonal* education.

Innovative Techniques

A good example of this effort is the work of Jack Canfield, the creator of the *Chicken Soup for the Soul* series. According to Canfield's website, he has taught millions of individuals his *formulas for success*. Canfield, who started out as a teacher, has touched the lives of countless educators.

In an interview with *Science of Mind* magazine, Canfield stated, "The purpose of New Age education is to help people manifest and express that essential Self."[3] This is apparent in his self-esteem programs. In the program's *Life Purpose Exercise*, you are supposed to "access your inner wisdom and find answers to your questions and solutions to your problems."[4] These exercises use what is referred to as the "closed eye process."[5] There can be little doubt that this is nothing more than standard meditation.

In the interview, Canfield presented his strategy for imparting these approaches into the public school system:

If we . . . point out to educators that they have an "essence" that can be invoked through "meditation" and "centering" exercises, they'll be put off by the buzzwords. But if we give them an experience that leaves them feeling better about themselves and each other, we can move them slowly into more and more internal states of awareness.[6]

This approach makes a lot of sense if you're trying to conceal meditation in a public school setting. All you have to tell the children is that they are doing some exercises to calm them down. Parents are not going to object to something like that. It would even be seen as being beneficial. However, principals might be concerned if they read *The Centering Book: Awareness Activities for Children, Parents and Teachers* by Gay Hendricks and Russell Wills. This book could be called a handbook for the New Age teacher. It says that since meditation and visualization are innovative techniques, the teacher may encounter trouble from school authorities when they are used in the classroom. As Jack Canfield said, it is sometimes expedient to change the terms. The book suggests that "quiet time" or just plain "relaxation" can be used as easily as meditation or centering. It adds that if school authorities object, they should be told these exercises "help children learn better by promoting relaxed alertness, and that they build positive self-image, and enhance creativity."[7]

Frequently when you look beneath the surface, you will find rather unconventional and controversial sources influence these activities, as you will see in the next sequence.

One Teacher's "Work"

The following example concerns a public school teacher involved with metaphysics who has self-published a small booklet titled *Attuning to Inner Guidance*. Her flier also claims that she trains other teachers how to "create a peaceable lifestyle in and out of school and ease anxiety, focus concentration, and apply superlearning concepts."[8]

In her booklet, she explains how she became involved in New Age consciousness. She suffered chronic physical pain in her left shoulder from a ski injury. When orthodox medicine failed to relieve her, she turned to alternative therapies for relief. One of them was Reiki, a New Age healing technique that will be discussed in more detail in the next chapter. As a result of her contact with Reiki, she had a transformation experience. She added, "What a Guide that shoulder was."[9]

In the section "Listening Deeply Within" the teacher presents her journal of channelings from her "Inner Teacher" (or higher self). The most revealing aspect of this journal is referred to as "My Work," where her Inner Teacher instructs her:

> Do not have concern. It is all happening. Make intuitional development [meditation] and Inner Guidance [direction by the Higher Self] commonplace. Get it out there for the everyman [sic]. . . Stay clear and as open as I am. [10]

I obtained a flier titled *Parenting With Hope, Health and Humor* presented by community school counselors and child development specialists at a local high school event. I found the teacher who wrote *Attuning to Inner Guidance* listed on the program under "Coping With Family Stress."

People have related stories to me of the influence of other such teachers in the most remote, rural, and most conservative of places. A friend of mine who attended a high school in an isolated desert town with a population of less than 350 told me about a science teacher who encouraged his biology classes to "focus on their energy centers" and meditate. Outside of class, he gave her his personal copies of several New Age books. He *truly believed* in the power and benefit of these activities and wanted to share them with his students.

Soul in the Classroom

Educator Rachel Kessler in her book, *The Soul of Education*, inadvertently makes the point of *For Many Shall Come in My Name* when she notes the interest of certain educators to involve students in meditation:

> Should modern public school children even *have*
> a soul? . . . Aren't questions of the soul private,
> spiritual matters best left at home? . . . To me, the
> most important challenge has always been not
> *whether* we can address spiritual development in
> secular schools but *how*.[11]

Kessler was aware that she was entering very controversial
waters with these approaches. She relates:

> Despite my fear that the community would
> misunderstand my efforts, I resolved to discuss
> this matter with parents, teachers, and students. I
> wanted to find a better understanding of the basic
> human need for transcendence and appropriate
> ways to address it in school.[12]

Once the way appeared open, Kessler would move in that
direction, but with caution. The reason for that caution is why
I have written this book. Kessler makes my point like few others
could have when she lays out the following concerns:

> If the parent community is supportive, however,
> meditation can lead to an altered state of
> consciousness that satisfies students' hunger for
> transcendence. . . . [I]f they choose to meditate,
> encourage only brief excursions into this realm .
> . . the still-forming ego of the child or adolescent
> is not strong enough to contain and safely process
> the *powerful energies* that may be released through
> prolonged meditative practice. (emphasis mine)[13]

To back this up, she then quotes in *her* book from a book
published by Theosophical Publishing House titled *The Secret
Life of Kids: An Exploration into Their Psychic Senses* written by J.
W. Peterson, who says:

[M]antras actually *work,* releasing energies that children literally are not equipped to handle.[14]

College "Ashrams"

Many people would find it hard to grasp that colleges and universities have become major purveyors of meditation practices. Because approximately 1,100 college students commit suicide every year in the U.S.,[15] students are told repeatedly that they have to have an outlet for their stress and burnout other than partying and drinking, so methods once thought too bizarre or esoteric are now being presented as the answer.

In one newspaper article on the subject called "Students Seek Quiet Within," the writer did an excellent job of revealing the broad scope of this trend. In a prominent state university over 1,000 students enrolled in "mind/body courses" in a single semester! One meditation teacher was quoted as saying of her students:

> [T]hey're invited to acknowledge that it's possible to switch the mind on and off. They don't always have to think, think, think.[16]

There are those who would say that just because students meditate, that doesn't mean they are New Agers. I address this very issue in depth in an upcoming chapter, but the fact remains that the core practice of New Age spirituality has indeed found its way into many institutions of higher learning. This has happened to the degree that you could call these colleges or universities *ashrams* or Hindu meditation centers. The reader would have to agree that a thousand students at just one university is a very large number.

Countless other colleges and universities are teaching meditation to students. Santa Fe Community College encourages students to meditate before exams as a way of "reducing the effects of stress on the body and mind."[17]

Yoga for Public School Students

Students in both elementary and high schools are being introduced to New Age meditation through yoga programs that are becoming increasingly popular. Mark Blanchard, a California yoga instructor teaches yoga to children at Colfax Elementary school in California. On his website, he explains: "I will be introducing yoga to all of the kids at the school as I donate a full yoga program."[18] Blanchard has been featured in many magazines such as *Family Circle* and *Seventeen* and has trained many actors and actresses (like Jennifer Lopez and Drew Barrymore). According to his website, he plans to "bring Progressive Power Yoga to as many places as I can around the states (as well as the globe) in the coming year."[19]

A program called YogaEd provides yoga classes under the heading of "Health/Wellness" programs for public schools. These programs take place in several states including California, Colorado, New York, Washington and Washington, DC.

Most likely yoga in schools is only going to become more popular. Why? According to one article, "Latest Way to Cut Grade School Stress: Yoga," yoga is supposed to help kids relax:

> Fourth graders at the Rosa Parks Elementary School have various classroom jobs: line leader, attendance taker, door locker, yoga monitor. "When you're mad you go do yoga and you feel much better," said Frederick Nettles, 10, a monitor who was coaching first graders in the intricacies of the "new moon," a forward-bending yoga posture. "It calms your nerves."[20]

Beyond the Traditional Classroom

The traditional classroom is not the only place a person can receive instruction these days. The past forty years have seen a tremendous rise in the *workshop* and *seminar* phenomenon. Many of these are conducted within corporations and institutions while others are held independently in hotel or motel conference rooms, community centers, and church or office recreation rooms.

In my research, I have seen countless brochures, pamphlets, and fliers promoting every conceivable type of New Age seminar. One promised to "give you the tools with which to fashion the life of your choosing, a life with new goals, new horizons, a new feeling of confidence and self-respect." Such promotions are full of expressions such as "your latent power," "your vast potential," or "the power of your inner being."[21]

Without exception, those who attend these events are promised deep satisfaction, prosperity, and health. The words and style may vary, but what they actually get is nothing more than courses in meditation.

The Learning Annex is a nationwide educational organization offering short term inexpensive courses to the general public. Their headquarters are in New York City, and they also have outlets in numerous other large cities. I found many interesting and practical courses in their catalog such as "How to Start Your Own Business" and "Increasing Your Listening Skills." However, I also found a copious number of courses and teachers presenting metaphysics.

When you look at the individuals listed as presenters, it's a menagerie of New Age superstars such as Wayne Dyer, Marianne Williamson, Deepak Chopra, well-known psychic Sylvia Browne, and the list goes on and on. Along with classes on Real Estate investing are classes titled "Tarot for the Curious," "Unleashing the Power of Wicca," "Ancient Wisdom for a Modern World," and "Your Sacred Self."

The Learning Annex has become so overtly and blatantly metaphysical that they even offer a class by psychic-medium J. Z. Knight who channels the widely known spirit guide who calls himself Ramtha. The public is invited to hear J. Z. Knight:

> . . . explor[e] the Extraordinary mind that exists
> within us all. Participants will discover how our

> normal minds construct our lives, and how to
> step outside of our reality to create extraordinary
> lives for ourselves. . . . His [Ramtha] powerful
> message of hope, freedom, and truth has already
> altered countless lives—none more powerfully and
> dramatically than JZ's own.[22]

The fact the Learning Annex now offers these classes online as well on location means that millions (which they claim on their website) of people can attend these classes no matter where they live in the world. And what draws so many is that the Learning Annex mixes those who are regarded as highly successful and respectable such as Donald Trump and television/radio personality Larry King with many of those who at one time would have been considered bizarre and outlandish. This in effect is *respect by association*. In other words, it is subconsciously transmitted to the general public that these things are no longer considered forbidden or weird and are now a normal part of society. *Time* magazine gave its stamp of approval by saying "The brash Learning Annex puts a fresh face on adult education."[23]

The Learning Annex is only a drop in the bucket. There are countless seminars, courses, and classes going on in communities, both large and small, continuously. Education does not just have to be in the public school system. It can be in any setting where something is taught to someone. Thus the New Age in education has far more influence than people understand. In fact, this influence is so pervasive that an entire book could be written just on that subject alone!

SIX

HOLISTIC HEALING AND ALTERNATIVE HEALTH

THE term *holistic* (also spelled *wholistic*) means *body, mind and spirit*. In other words, it includes the makeup of the *whole* person. According to this perspective, to achieve optimal health and well-being, all three aspects of the person have to be working smoothly. If one aspect is out of balance, the whole human machine is out of balance. Holistic health practitioners claim their job is to restore balance between the physical, mental, and spiritual elements of their patients. One holistic health source explains:

> All agree that the healing is for body, mind, and spirit, and that physical healing is only an entry point for higher spiritual teachings.[1]

Expanding in popularity from the late 1960s, the holistic health field has also been referred to as the *alternative* health movement. In the past, holistic practitioners have tended to be *counterculture* types. Books and catalogs on holistic health had the Woodstock generation look about them. Today the alternative health field has grown into a major industry that is gaining respect and acceptance.

Mainstream health organizations are incorporating holistic methods into their procedures at an ever increasing rate. In much the same way that New Age beliefs and techniques are creeping into business and education, so individuals who have become transformed are actively trying to bring these methods into their respective health fields. One New Age publication put it very well in saying:

> The wholistic model derives its view of health from
> the same core values that animate other segments
> of New Age life.[2]

The concept is that the path to true spiritual well-being is connecting with one's *higher wisdom* or true inner being. You do not have to look into the holistic health movement very deeply to realize that the underlying elements are nothing more than the teachings of the Ancient Wisdom.

The holistic health field is multi-faceted. It incorporates much that is practical and useful. Nutrition, herbs, chiropractic, and massage are some of the practices found in holistic health that have no direct connection with New Age spirituality. Acupressure/acupuncture is more controversial. The subject matter for this chapter primarily concerns energy healing, crystal work, and meditation as stress reduction therapy—categories that could be classified as *transformational* in nature.

Energy Healing

In the book, *Forever Fit*, Cher speaks of a friend of hers who is a metaphysical "healer":

> She heals with her hands and, boy, if she puts her
> hands on you, you know you've been touched. Even

near your body you feel it. It's simply unbelievable. But she is truly tuned in to some kind of higher power.[3]

Occultists believe that man has more than one body, that there are other invisible *bodies* superimposed on the physical body. They refer to one of these as the *etheric body* and believe there lies within it energy centers called *chakras* (pronounced shock-ras). The term chakra means *whirling wheel* in Sanskrit, the ancient Hindu language. They were seen by those with clairvoyant powers as spinning balls of psychic energy. It is taught that there are seven chakras, which start at the base of the spine and end at the crown chakra at the top of the head.

Each chakra is supposed to have a different function corresponding to certain levels of awareness. The chakras act as conduits or conductors for what is called *kundalini* or *serpent energy*. They say this force lies coiled but dormant at the base of the spine like a snake. When awakened during meditation, it is supposed to travel up the spine activating each chakra as it surges upward. When the kundalini force hits the crown chakra, the person experiences *enlightenment* or Self-realization. This mystical current results in the person *knowing* himself to be God. That is why kundalini is sometimes referred to as the *divine energy*. According to New Age proponents, all meditative methods involve energy and power, and the greater the power, the greater the experience.

Basically, what all energy healing entails is opening up the chakras through meditation or transferring the kundalini power from someone already attuned to it:

> At the sixth chakra, a person opens to a higher level
> of intuition and inner guidance. At the seventh, the
> person feels a sense of merging with Spirit.[4]

I want people to know that energy healing is fundamentally supernatural in nature. It is not based on something physically tangible as massage or chiropractic. The chakras are not something you can open up surgically and look at like you can the physical organs like the heart or spleen.

The *chakra system* is the basis for virtually all energy-healing techniques. In energy-healing, the power is channeled into the patient, thus bringing about the desired *wellness* and *wholeness* of the person receiving it. Currently, there are a number of energy-healing systems. Although they have different names, the energy that they use is from the same source.

Reiki

One of the fastest growing New Age healing techniques being used today is *Reiki,* (pronounced ray-key), a Japanese word which translates *universal life energy* or *God* energy. It has also been referred to as *the Radiance Technique*. Reiki is an ancient Tibetan healing system which was *rediscovered* by a Japanese man in the 1880s and has only recently been brought to the West.

The technique consists of placing the hands on the recipient and then activating the energy to *flow through* the practitioner into the recipient. One practitioner describes the experience in the following way:

> When doing it, I become a channel through which this force, this juice of the universe, comes pouring from my palms into the body of the person I am touching, sometimes lightly, almost imperceptibly, sometimes in famished sucking drafts. I get it even as I'm giving it. It surrounds the two of us, patient and practitioner.[5]

One obtains this power to perform Reiki by being *attuned* by a Reiki master. This is done in four sessions in which the master activates the chakras, creating an open channel for the energy. The attunement process is not made known for general information, but is held in secrecy for only those being initiated.

One of the main reasons Reiki has become so popular is its apparently pleasurable experience. Those who have experienced Reiki report feeling a powerful sense of warmth and security. One woman, now a Reiki master, remarked after her first encounter: "I don't know what this is you've got but I just have to have it."[6] People don't make such comments unless there is an appeal involved. A successful business woman gives Reiki the following praise:

> Reiki should be available through every medical, chiropractic and mental health facility in this country. Your fees are a small price to pay for such impressive results. I don't know how Reiki works, but it works; that's all that counts in my book.[7]

New Age teaching is that once someone is attuned he or she can never lose the power; it is for life. Even distance is not a barrier for the Reiki energy, for the channeler may engage in something called *absentee healing,* in which the energy is *sent* over long distances, even thousands of miles.

One master relates:

> Just by having the name or an object of the person or perhaps even a picture in your hand, you can send Reiki to them to wherever they are in the world.[8]

Over *one million* people are practicing Reiki in the United States alone today.[9] In many cases, these are people who treat or work with others on a therapeutic basis, such as health professionals, body workers, chiropractors, and counselors. Despite its bizarre and unconventional nature, Reiki has struck a chord with an incredible number of average people. In Europe alone, the number of people accepting Reiki is very impressive. One Reiki master claims that in the thirteen years she lived in Europe she alone initiated 45,000 people into Reiki as channelers.[10]

What Reiki is *really* about is using this power to transform others into New Age consciousness. As one Reiki leader states:

> [I]t also makes a level of spiritual transformation available to non-meditators, that is usually reserved for those with a meditative path.[11]

Statements like this reveal that Reiki is in line with all the other New Age transformation efforts. It changes the way people *perceive reality.* Most practitioners acknowledge the truth of this. A German Reiki channeler makes this comment:

> It frequently happens that patients will come into contact with new ideas after a few Reiki treatments. Some will start doing yoga or autogenous training or start to meditate or practise [sic] some other kind of spiritual method. . . . Fundamental changes will set in and new things will start to develop. You will find it easier to cast off old, outlived structures and you will notice that you are being led and guided more and more.[12]

What concerns me is that Reiki apparently can be combined with regular massage techniques without the recipient even knowing it. A letter in the *Reiki Journal* reveals:

> Reiki is a whole new experience when used in my massage therapy practice. Massage, I thought, would be an excellent tool to spread the radiance of this universal energy and a client would benefit and really *not realize what a wonderful growth was happening in his or her being* (emphasis mine).[13]

Of all the New Age practices and modalities, Reiki holds the title to being the most intriguing and perhaps eerie one. This is brought out in the following observations made by one of the leading Reiki masters in the country. He reveals:

> When I looked psychically at the energy, I could
> often see it as thousands of small particles of light,
> like "corpuscles" filled with radiant Reiki energy
> flowing through me and out of my hands. It was
> as though these Reiki "corpuscles" of light had a
> purpose and intelligence.[14]

Since Reiki is not something taught intellectually even children can be brought into it. In one Reiki magazine, I found an ad that was offering a *Children's Reiki Handbook: A Guide to Energy Healing for Kids*. The book is described as a "guide that provides kids with what they need to prepare for their first Reiki Attunement."[15]

Therapeutic Touch

Therapeutic touch is another widespread healing technique. This method was developed and promoted by Dr. Delores Krieger, a professor of nursing at New York University.

While Reiki is obtained by being attuned by a master, therapeutic touch is acquired by standard metaphysical meditation commonly referred to as *centering*. Teachers of therapeutic touch readily acknowledge that "centering is probably the most important part of the entire process."[16]

A practitioner relates that when she first encountered therapeutic touch in graduate nursing school, it was "the craziest, kookiest stuff I'd ever seen or heard." This skepticism did not last. She explains:

> I got through the semester, though, and in the process
> Dr. Krieger performed the procedure on me. It was
> then I knew something very real was going on, so I
> continued to learn about it, and practice it.[17]

Like the others, she attributes this power to "the individual Higher Self"[18] and feels that this type of healing is not just for the body, but is also "very spiritual."[19]

Crystals

Although it may appear to be a fad to the average person, the metaphysical use of quartz crystal, like most New Age practices, dates back to early history. Its usage is found in virtually all occult traditions. Today, crystals are being used by New Agers for basically two reasons—to enhance their meditation and to store energy. They say that just having a crystal in their presence while they meditate deepens their level of consciousness and resulting experiences are more powerful.

Metaphysicians will tell you that the crystals by themselves contain no power or ability. They function as *amplifiers* for the energy during meditation. One of them relates:

> An interesting phenomenon happens when you begin to work with crystals—for whatever reason. You will start becoming aware of an energy or force greater than what you presently contain. This force has been called your Higher Self, and it encompasses "that which you are capable of becoming." It is your perfected self. Quartz crystals, in their wonderfully helpful way, will help you tune into this higher aspect of yourself.[20]

These energies are then used by the crystal healer to bring about supposed physical, mental, and spiritual health in the patient. As with Reiki, therapeutic touch, and other energy healing techniques, crystal work is also based on the chakra system. One practitioner reveals:

> Crystal work, psychic work, healing work, or any work of a metaphysical nature, uses the higher chakras or energy centers; the third eye, crown, throat and/or heart center.[21]

Hands of Light

In her highly acclaimed book, *Hands of Light*, healer Barbara Ann Brennan lays out the dynamics of such practices as Reiki and therapeutic touch.

A color photo in her book shows a drawn picture of a woman doing energy healing on another woman. On each side of the healer are two faceless figures that fit the description of the *beings of light* spoken of in my first chapter. The picture reveals that the power is coming from the two "entities" whom Brennan describes as "the guides."[22] Brennan explains that:

> The healer must first open and align herself with the cosmic forces. This means not only just before the healing, but in her life in general.[23]

These "cosmic forces" also have names. Brennan tells of an exchange between herself and a spirit being (who calls himself "Heyoan") who reveals to her: "Enlightenment is the goal; healing is a by-product."[24] What he meant by this is that the forces behind energy healing are really pushing the *man-is-God* view and any physical benefits are just the bait.

Anyone considering undergoing *any* chakra-based energy therapy should first seriously consider Brennan's sobering revelation that "I and Heyoan are one."[25]

Stress Management

Stress is believed to be one of the leading causes of illness in America today. Millions of people suffer from disorders such as headaches, insomnia, nerves, and stomach problems because of excessive stress in their lives. In response to this situation, an army of practitioners have come forward to teach *relaxation skills* and *stress reduction techniques* to the afflicted millions. A newspaper article proclaims:

> Once a practice that appealed mostly to mystics and
> occult followers, meditation now is reaching the
> USA's mainstream.... The medical establishment
> now recognizes the value of meditation and other
> mind-over-body states in dealing with stress-related
> illnesses.[26]

Does all meditation lead to New Age mysticism? Can a person meditate *without* having a metaphysical motive? Can it be done just to relax and get rid of tension without any *spiritual* side effects? These are legitimate questions. Suppose a company brings in a *stress specialist* to give a seminar and all employees are required to attend. What if a doctor prescribes meditation to relieve migraine headaches? Say an aerobics instructor has the class lie on their backs, close their eyes and do breathing exercises. *Is* there such a thing as neutral meditation?

I once asked John Klimo (who wrote what has been called the definitive book on channeling) if the millions of people meditating for stress reduction could become transformed as a result. His response almost sent me through the ceiling! "Most certainly," he replied with marked enthusiasm. Being a channeler himself he viewed the possibility of this with great expectation.

His optimism was well-founded. When the meditation techniques used in stress reduction are compared to the meditation used in New Age spirituality, it is clear to see they are basically the same. Both use either the breathing or mantra method to still the mind. A blank state of mind is all that is necessary for contact to occur.

Some well-known channelers became so because meditation catapulted them into the world of spirit entities. Jach Pursel, who channels the immensely popular "Lazaris," (see chapter two), explains how this *entity* first came to him:

> Early evening. Sitting on the bed, plumped up in
> pillows, I am preparing to meditate (ha!). I am going
> to seek insight (ha!) to help guide our lives. . . .

Two hours later, Peny [his wife] didn't hear my sheepish apology for having dozed off. She was excitedly tumbling over words trying to tell me that an entity had spoken through me. She thought I had fallen asleep again, too. This time, however, my head didn't bob, so she waited. Some minutes passed, and then a deep, resonant voice began where mine had left off. The answers, however, were powerful, not of the caliber of mine. She listened. She wrote as fast as she could. . . .

The entity explained that he was Lazaris! . . . Lazaris requested two weeks of our time to finalize the necessary adjustments so he could "channel" through me. He provided Peny with a simple, but detailed, method I should use to enter trance more easily. He assured her that this experience would never be detrimental, that although he had neither a body nor time, he appreciated that we did, and he would never abuse either.[27]

Kevin Ryerson (featured in Shirley MacLaine's book and television movie *Out on a Limb*) also got into channeling by accident. He joined a meditation group hoping that he could tap into some inner reservoir of creativity just as many in the business world are now doing. He relates:

When I entered this group, I had no intention or expectation of becoming a trance medium. But after six months, in the course of one of our sessions, I entered into a "spontaneous channeling state," as I refer to it now.[28]

John Randolph Price, founder of the Quartus Foundation and instigator of the December 3rd World Healing Day Meditation, also became involved in metaphysics through this route. He reveals:

Back when I was in the business world, the American
Management Association put out a little book on
meditation, which indicated that meditation was
a way to attain peace of mind and reduce stress in
a corporate environment. So I decided I'd try it.
. . . I learned that I could go into meditation as a
human being, and within a matter of minutes, have
transcended my sense of humanness. I discovered
how to come into a new sphere of consciousness.
Consciousness actually *shifts*, and you move into
a realm you may not have even known existed.[29]

So, can meditation be done without potential spiritual side
effects? For those who still say yes, give ear to the following:

In alpha [meditative state] the mind opens up to
nonordinary forms of communication, such as
telepathy, clairvoyance, and precognition ... In
alpha the rational filters that process ordinary
reality *are weakened or removed,* and the mind is
receptive to nonordinary realities. (emphasis mine)[30]

You must be willing to slow down, to stop and just
be quiet. It is into this quiet space [meditation], not
the noisy one, that Spirit enters. Make a sacred
space for your High Self to enter by being silent
and willing to listen, willing to simply BE. This
attracts your superconscious essence like a magnet.
(emphasis mine)[31]

First and foremost, almost all mediums agree on
the significance and the importance of regular
daily meditation. This single practice, above all
others, is no doubt the very shaft that drives the
wheel of development.[32]

Even though meditation can bring you seeming peace of
mind and improved health, I believe it is evident, by the accounts

just given, that those who engage in it may find themselves in similar circumstances. According to New Ager Betty Bethards, "Meditation can, and does, change your life because it changes *you*."[33] Ken Wilber, another New Age writer and expert in the field of higher consciousness, aptly puts it:

> If you're doing meditation correctly, *you're* in for some very rough and frightening times. Meditation as a relaxation response is a joke.[34]

I understand the bizarre implications of what I am trying to convey and certainly can see where a skeptic might laugh at such accusations. But evidence to the contrary is abundant. In 1996, *Time* magazine actually did an article on just such a reality. The article, called "Ambushed By Spirituality" was written by a Hollywood studio executive and producer who described himself as "the last guy you'd figure would go spiritual on you."[35] Marty Kaplin, explained how he "stumbled" onto "meditation" to keep from grinding his teeth when he became stressed. The following backs up my bold assertion:

> I got more from mind-body medicine than I bargained for. I got religion. . . . The spirituality of it ambushed me. Unwittingly, I was engaging in a practice [meditation] that has been at the heart of religious mysticism for millenniums. . . . Now I know there is a consciousness that transcends science, a consciousness toward which our species is sputteringly evolving.[36]

Nathaniel Mead, another authority that was honest and open about the *side effects* of simple meditation practice, echoed what Ken Wilber warned about. In a natural health magazine, Mead states:

> One source of meditation problems comes from the attempt to turn a powerful, psychological technique

into a simple physical therapy. When a meditator is led to expect stress reduction and instead comes face to face with his true self, the result can be anything but relaxing.[37]

But in spite of the dangers and risks, meditation continues to be promoted by those in the alternative health profession.

The prestigious Mayo Clinic has put its stamp of approval on meditation as well, in its book *The Mayo Clinic Book of Alternative Medicine*. The book gives the green light by stating:

> Today many people use meditation for health and wellness purposes. In meditation, a person focuses attention on his or her breathing, or on repeating a word, phrase or sound in order to suspend the stream of thoughts that normally occupies the conscious mind. . . . Meditation may be used to treat a number of problems, including anxiety, pain, depression, stress and insomnia.[38]

The book then devotes an entire page with step-by-step instructions on how to meditate. These instructions are the exact same type of meditation that you have been reading about in my book (i.e., focus on the breath and repetition of words and phrases). The Mayo Clinic's acceptance of Eastern-style meditation is an excellent barometer for how wide-spread meditation has become in respectable society. And with the explosion of stress and anxiety in Western culture and the promotion of meditative techniques by such reputable institutions as the Mayo Clinic, this will neutralize any opposition people may have to meditation based on the perception of it being unorthodox. In essence, meditation is now for the masses!

SEVEN

NEW AGE IN ARTS AND MEDIA

WE live in a culture where television, movies, the printed page, and now the Internet wield a great influence. And perhaps more than any other movement, the New Age movement has experienced stupendous growth because of these vehicles of communication. It is obvious to even the most casual observer that New Age themes are present in both news and entertainment. Even the smallest influence can be a step in the process of fulfilling this obvious paradigm shift. Through constant exposure to New Age concepts, people will be less likely to view them as weird or off-beat. Familiarity has enabled the public to accept them as the norm and give their stamp of approval.

Newspapers and Free Publications

It is not only common to find feature articles with New Age themes in daily newspapers, it is most likely that every issue, especially those papers in metropolitan areas, will have at least one article with New Age emphasis. The subjects most often covered are meditation, yoga, Reiki and other forms of meta-physical healing, along with special New Age events and profiles of certain New Age individuals who are active in the community.

One regional newspaper that serves an area of several million people did a feature article on a New Age healer in the community. It was featured under the heading of "Wellness and Spirituality." The piece has a very affirming tone to it, as the writer discloses:

> Today, a growing number of Americans are turning to psychics—or intuitives—as a way to achieve spiritual wellness. The phrase "mind-body-spirit connection" was virtually unheard of ten years ago. Today, it's almost a cliche', the subject of thousands of books, classes and lectures. Even Kaiser Permanente, one of the country's largest traditional HMOs, promotes the concept.[1]

The healer herself is presented in ways that could spark the interest of the non-metaphysical oriented reader. She assures:

> Meditation and self-reflection are wonderful tools to tap into our own consciousness as well as the greater consciousness that exists.[2]

In addition to mainstream newspapers, New Age articles are also found in community newspapers and resource guides. These newspapers offer what's new around town in art, entertainment, food, music, and local social and political issues.

One newspaper, *Willamette Week Online* (Portland, Oregon) advertises local New Age businesses and upcoming metaphysical workshops/seminars. In just one week's time, there are over seventy Reiki ads, over 700 listings for yoga, including "Yoga for Kids" and "Couples Kundalini Class." Other listings include virtually every New Age topic imaginable from astrology to Zen.[3]

Other types of free resource guides are those that focus only on New Age topics. These guides can be found in bookstores, metaphysical centers, holistic clinics, vegetarian restaurants, music stores, fitness centers, community colleges, universities, some retail outlets, and natural food stores.

Magazines

New Age publications, mainstream magazines, and tabloids also expose the public to New Age thought. Some of the more prominent outright New Age publications include: *Yoga Journal* (cir. 1,000,000), *Magical Blend* (cir. 100,000), *Spirituality & Health* (cir. 85,000), *Science of Mind*, and *Light of Consciousness*.

These magazines are sold in newsstands, bookstores, supermarkets, metaphysical outlets, health food stores, and most can be viewed on the Internet. Feature articles run the gamut of the metaphysical spectrum. Some topics included are interviews with New Age personalities, viewpoints on various meditation techniques, book reviews, and listings of events. People who read these publications are usually already acquainted with New Age beliefs.

Mainstream magazines commonly publish articles with New Age themes. Depending on the type of magazine and what is being covered, these articles vary in the way New Age topics are treated. For example, stories on crystals are generally respectful; channelers usually get slammed; articles on meditation and holistic health are almost always treated favorably, especially when presented in a therapeutic context.

It's apparent that many magazine articles are openly metaphysical. One such example is the May/June 2004 issue of *Spirituality & Health* magazine. An article titled "Four Basic Spiritual Practices to Increase Positive Energy" begins:

> In a quiet place, sit in a comfortable position. Turn off beepers and phones; shut the door. Eyes closed, focus on your breath, each inhalation and exhalation. If thoughts come and go; return your awareness to your breath. Visualize thoughts as

clouds drifting by; just let them pass. Then gently place your palm over your heart chakra (in your mid-chest), and visualize what connects you to spirit —a beautiful dawn, an image of Jesus or the Buddha, a sense of love. Observe all sensations in the heart area—heat, tingling, expansion, bliss. Let this positive energy flow through your body.[4]

Such articles can desensitize people to the mystical realm and even lead them into practicing it also.

The least credible source of influence are the gossip tabloids. Anyone glancing through them can't help noticing the barrage of stories on psychics, astrology, ghosts, UFOs, secret powers, and the like. Still, I suspect they are more influential than people realize.

Books

As anyone knows, books have been one of the major avenues   that any movement uses to promote its ideas and practices. The New Age is no exception. Starting in the mid 1970s, the best seller lists have been saturated and sometimes even dominated by Aquarian titles. As one who has followed this trend for 22 years, I can attest to the immense popularity of books on this subject. For the most part, New Age titles are geared toward those who want to improve their lives. Some of the top sellers have had such names as "You Can Heal Your Life" or "The Seven Spiritual Laws Of Success." This approach has been observed by those in academic circles. Professor James A. Herrick writes of this phenomenon:

> [B]ookstores have emerged as the most important centers of unchurched [New Age] spirituality. . . . The boundaries of American religion are clearly being redrawn. The suppliers of unchurched spirituality are no longer seen as addressing a small group of "kooks" who just don't fit into respectable American society.[5]

The prestigious magazine, *Publishers Weekly*, did a seven page article on the impact of New Age books in society. The article, called "Casting a Wider Spell," states:

> After years on the fringes, New Age—which includes some alternative health, addiction and recovery, psychology and spirituality titles, as well as books on Eastern traditions—may finally be approaching the middle of the road. . . . "New Age is no longer becoming main stream; it is main stream," says Katie McMillan, publicity manager at Inner Ocean Publishing Company.[6]

Without a doubt, your local shopping-mall bookstore is proof that a metaphysical paradigm shift is taking place. The psychology, self-help, philosophy, business, religious, health, and physical fitness sections all contain numerous books pushing meditation, visualization, and hypnosis as the keys to success and problem solving. The level of metaphysical content in these areas is truly astounding. In fact, this was the major indication to me, at the outset of my research, that the New Age movement is something to be taken seriously.

Today, something even more astounding has taken place. More and more bookstores are getting rid of their "New Age" sections and replacing them with sections such as "Spirituality" or "Metaphysical." And often Christianity and other religions have been absorbed into these sections. The mystical element is so pervasive that it is blending in with every religious tradition. What's more, New Age Thought is popping up in books on every subject. It has just become the way books are written. And now that book outlets like Barnes & Noble and Borders are selling such books, including the ones just on metaphysical subjects (Yoga, reincarnation, TM, astrology, etc.), there are fewer and fewer bookstores that are designated as just New Age bookstores.

Harry Potter

There are probably very few people in the western world who haven't heard of the Harry Potter book series phenomenon. Not just millions, but tens of millions of adults, adolescents, and children have read these books or seen the movie versions of them. Going by the numbers of the books that have been purchased, few under 25 have not been influenced to some degree by the adventures of this boy wizard. And many ask, what is wrong with that?

The Potter series, though fiction in the technical sense, does make a very real connection to the realm of metaphysics in one spot specifically. In the book called *Harry Potter and the Prisoner of Azkaban*, one of the main characters, a professor, tells her class that they will learn divination or *see into the future*. It's at this point that the book departs from the world of *make believe*, and enters into the actual teachings of Wicca (witchcraft). The teacher informs the students:

> Crystal gazing is a particularly refined art. . . . We shall start by practicing relaxing the conscious mind and external eyes, . . . so as to clear the Inner Eye and the superconscious.[7]

All one has to do is type in the word "superconscious" on Google on the Internet and see just how highly promoted that term is. It comes up nearly 130,000 times! Keep in mind, this term is used specifically within the context of metaphysics, and is never used in a non-metaphysical sense. What this means is that any impressionable young person who reads this term, could become more open and comfortable with the mystical realm in real life.

This is what you would be taught if you attended a *real* school of witchcraft. Relaxing the conscious mind is, of course, meditation, and the Inner Eye is an occult term used for the Third eye chakra from which all psychic powers, such as divination, spring. But the absolute clincher is the term "superconscious." If you were to ask any New Age teacher, guru, or practitioner what the "superconscious"* is, you would get the same answer—it's the New Age concept of God. In fact, *Buckland's Complete Book Of Witchcraft* actually uses the term "Superconsciousness" in reference to what or to whom witches tune into during meditation.[8]

There is another more subtle, yet perhaps more far-reaching aspect to the Potter books. In the series, those people who are "non-magical" or ordinary are called "muggles." They are portrayed as dull, backward, and lacking in personality. It is inferred that if you are a "muggle," you are living an inferior and unsatisfying life. Now if there were no such thing as "muggles" this comparison would be meaningless. How can you feel bad about being something that doesn't exist? But, as I have already shown, *The Prisoner of Azkaban* presents *real witchcraft*. So then, not to have access to the "superconscious" makes one a "muggle," (i.e., a non-mystic). This means that the spiritual beliefs of potentially millions of young people, many of them from conservative homes too, may be altered if they pick up this outlook, even subconsciously; thus the Potter books may be a highly effective tool in giving the New Age movement a boost that is unimaginable. It will implant in the minds of multitudes that to fail to embrace mysticism makes you, well, muggle-like.

Television

If readers would hear the term New Age in television, they would most likely relate it to popular shows such as "Medium," about a psychic housewife, or "Crossing Over," a show about psychic Jonathan Edward, or most likely Montel Williams' talk show, which regularly features best selling author and psychic Sylvia Browne. But the real situation is far more profound in scope and impact. You could even use the term *televangelist* to describe the nature of what I want to convey. The two individuals

---

*Please see pages 21, 42, and 86 for context of this term.

that I will discuss here may not be widely viewed in this manner, but that is in essence what they are.

The first one is Oprah Winfrey, a name that has been a household word for many years. She has a regular audience of 49 million viewers in 121 countries. One article put this in the context of a spiritual outreach. It describes her as having a "global pulpit"[10] and as being "a symbol and prophetess for the new American religion."[11] Oprah herself refers to her show as "my ministry."[12] As to how this came about, the article reveals that "her emergence as a spiritual force began in the 1994-95 season when she separated herself from the more conventional TV talk show hosts."[13] From that time on, she used her show as a platform for virtually every New Age figure around. She even launched a few of them from obscurity to national prominence such as Marianne Williamson. The reason for this is that she shares their views on God, and wants to impart this to her viewers. Referring to God as *spirit*, she states:

> It exists in all things, all the time. It is the essence
> of who you are. You are spirit expressing itself.[14]

Another figure who commands an enormous television audience is Wayne Dyer. He is usually aired on public television stations during their seasonal pledge drives. His shows are done in front of a large theater audience in which he expounds on such lofty themes as "The Power of Intention" or "Inspiration." Dyer, who is commonly called the "father of motivation,"[15] could also be called the Billy Graham of the New Age movement. His PBS specials, which have been airing for years, reach perhaps as many viewers as Oprah's show does. Dyer has also sold fifty million copies of his numerous books. In essence, his message is identical to Oprah's:

> [L]iving as a spiritual being involves going beyond your
> five senses, meditating . . . in order that your invisible
> Divine Guidance is always there steering your life.[16]

What motivates both Oprah Winfrey and Wayne Dyer is the goal that underlies the whole New Age movement, which is to bring the *Age of Aquarius* (i.e., New Age) into reality. Both of them believe, as Dyer notes:

> When enough of us align in a certain way, reaching a critical mass, then the rest of us will begin to be affected and align that way also.[17]

Radio

Most large cities have talk shows that feature both local and national New Agers. Many times, while listening to a radio talk show, I have heard various guests expound on the dynamics of New Age consciousness.

One of the most popular and far-reaching radio programs is New Dimensions Media. This San Francisco-based talk show is heard all across the country on scores of FM stations as well as on Satellite radio, which makes it available around the world. The program used to begin with a catchy violin tune as you heard a pleasant male voice say, "It is only through a change of consciousness that the world will be transformed." Guests on the show have included the most influential New Age speakers and writers of our time, some of which are Willis Harman, Marianne Williamson, Barbara Marx Hubbard, and Wayne Dyer. *Conscious evolutionist* Barbara Marx Hubbard describes her view of the higher self:

> You all have the same master from within. That master is me, your higher self, the Christ within each of you who is, right now, hearing the same vision of the future, despite all differences of language and culture.[18]

Marx Hubbard has been a guest on New Dimensions radio several times with program titles like: "Hope for the Universal Human," "Conscious Evolution," and the "Co-Creative Adventure," all of which are New Age themes.

In one New Dimensions show titled "A World of Wizards," New Age proponent Deepak Chopra talked about "[h]ow we are the creators of material reality" and discussed "[t]he attributes of enlightenment."[18] Chopra, a strong advocate for mantric meditation says:

> Once a person becomes comfortable with simply sitting quietly and focusing on breathing, I recommend adding a mantra, which creates a mental environment that will allow you to *expand your consciousness*. (emphasis mine)[19]

It is this "consciousness" that New Dimensions, and other radio programs like it, hope to "expand" by being a voice for the Ancient Wisdom, which New Agers believe is the answer to all personal and planetary problems.

New Age Music

New Age music is most often soft, melodic, non-percussion, non-lyrical music that is very conducive to meditation. Entertainment was not the motive of the musical artists when they began to promote this genre in the 1970s. They wanted to create music that would convey their spiritual outlook. It is interesting to note that much of New Age music is admittedly *channeled* from the higher self or spirit masters.

New Age music has become a major interest in the music industry. It even has its own category at the Grammy Awards. The 2005 Grammy Award for Best New Age Album was Paul Winter for his album titled *Silver Solstice*. Winter considers his music to be a celebration in honor of the earth and the winter and summer *solstices*.

New Age music's increasing popularity will no doubt draw many listeners into the metaphysical belief system that underlies its soft, hypnotic melodies.

Movies

Movies are such an enjoyable form of entertainment because they give people a chance to look at life from a different viewpoint. The New Age movement is not missing this opportunity for influence at all. In fact, over the last twenty years numerous films have been released that incorporate New Age themes, and this trend is not abating. For those knowledgeable of the New Age, it is fairly simple to catch metaphysical themes or references in many of these films. And some of them are downright blatant.

In 2004, a film titled *What the Bleep Do We Know?* was released. The movie grossed over eleven million dollars and was a documentary/story showing the connection between science and mysticism, and the conclusion that God or divinity is within each human being. One newspaper did a cover story on the film, stating:

> The most intriguing movie of 2004 has nothing to do with George W. Bush, Hogwarts School of Witchcraft and Wizardry, or killer zombies. No, the topic is metaphysics—and the movie is *What the Bleep Do We Know?*
>
> The premise may sound outlandish, but the film has become a cult classic. More than 60,000 people saw it at the Bagdad Theater, where it played for 18 weeks. "It's been a huge success," says Peter Boicourt, the film buyer for McMenamins theaters. "We've *never* played a film that long before."[20]

The article goes on to say that the movie is the result of a channeled work by Ramtha, a mighty warrior-spirit from Atlantis.

In 2005, another pro-New Age movie, *Bee Season*, hit the theaters. Richard Gere (a Hollywood movie actor) played the father of a precocious eleven year old, who performed in spelling bees. In the movie, Gere teaches his daughter how to meditate. In one scene, she goes into a Kundalini trance and falls to the floor convulsing. The movie had many other New Age connotations also, such as the older brother joining an Eastern religious group.

Other recent movies have been along the same lines as *Bee Season*. In 2006 alone, there were a number of titles including the film about New Ager Neale Donald Walsch, named after his book series *Conversations with God* and *the Celestine Prophecy* (named after James Redfield's very popular book). On the *Celestine Prophecy* website, the description of the movie reads:

> [A] spiritual adventure film chronicling the discovery of ancient scrolls in the rainforests of Peru. The prophecy and its nine key insights predict a worldwide awakening, arising within all religious traditions, that moves humanity toward a deeper experience of spirituality.[21]

This "worldwide awakening" is exactly what I am talking about in this book. New Agers believe that as society is molded by such beliefs, there will indeed be a great awakening.

Star Wars

Of all the New Age movies released, the granddaddy of them all has been the *Star Wars* series by George Lucas. Although they are entertainment fiction, all the movies (*Star Wars*, *The Empire Strikes Back*, and *Return of the Jedi*, etc.) could not be any bolder in their presentation of metaphysical proclivities. The films center around characters who are presented as "Jedi Knights." A Jedi Knight is someone who controls the "Force," which is said to be the basic power of the universe. It is neutral and can be used for good or evil, depending on the will of the Jedi Knight. Obe-Wan Kenobi is a good Jedi, while Darth Vader is an evil one. In the middle of this saga is a young man, Luke Skywalker, who, along with an assortment of bizarre and loveable characters, sides with the good side of the Force. Virtually all the main elements of New Age thought are found in the *Star Wars* stories. The Force is the Universal Mind (another word for the higher self), and Jedi Knights are nothing less than traditional occultists (individuals trained in hidden wisdom who have command of mystical powers). When Luke Skywalker needed to be trained in the Force, he was sent to a remote planet to find Yoda, a Jedi master. Occultists have traditionally dwelt in remote places because they needed the solitude for meditating, and Yoda is no exception as his character clearly reveals

One particular scene from *The Empire Strikes Back* embodies the main message of these films. Luke has made contact with Yoda and is undergoing a period of training or initiation. He is trying to raise a crashed spaceship out of the swamp with his "inner powers," but he does not succeed. Yoda then closes his eyes (in meditation) and with the power of the Force, lifts the spaceship out of the muck and onto the bank.

"I don't believe it," Luke says in dismay.

"That is why you failed,"[22] Yoda replies with a wise look.

The underlying message is that we can create our own reality when we master our inner powers and nothing is impossible when the power of the will is aligned with the higher self (or "the Force" as it is called here).

Meditation is also presented as the method to achieve this power. "Tune out your thoughts, let the Force take over," Obe-Wan tells Luke in *Star Wars*. At the end of the movie, Obe-Wan (now speaking as a spirit guide) tells Luke, "You don't need your instruments. Let the Force take over."[23]

George Lucas, the creator and producer of *Star Wars* is very much a devotee of Eastern spirituality. It is clear he saw his movies as a way to evangelize the public and entertain them at the same time. In one very revealing interview, he disclosed:

> I was raised Methodist. Now let's say I'm spiritual.
> It's Marin County. We're all Buddhists up here.[24]

The Internet

Probably no other medium has hastened the expansion of the New Age movement as much as the Internet. Millions of websites espouse New Age practices, theologies, and personalities, bringing the New Age into virtually every home in America. Anyone who has a computer (which is the majority of people in the Western world today), not only can read about the New Age they can participate in the New Age as well. There are online labyrinths that give web visitors a virtual meditative experience as they *walk* the labyrinth. Videos can be watched that offer yoga instruction and other meditation practices online. Where not too long ago a person had to travel out of his or her home to attend a seminar or workshop, now the same thing can be learned in the comfort of the home. There is even music to meditate by on some websites.

A highly popular website is the Witch's Voice. This site has been in existence since 1997 (a long time for the relatively new Internet).[25] A Google search shows that this site has over 268,000 listings on the Internet.

Any teenager who lives in a remote rural area now has as much access to a vast body of knowledge on Wicca as if he or she lived

	2007	2011
Yoga	66,800,000	220,000,000
Meditation	43,200,000	117,000,000
New Age	35,000,000	63,000,000
Astrology	32,300,000	70,500,000
Tarot	24,300,000	82,300,000
Buddhism	18,000,000	43,900,000
Reiki	17,800,000	36,800,000
Mysticism	7,280,000	14,600,000
Wicca	6,400,000	13,400,000
Reincarnation	5,700,000	17,800,000
Kabbalah	3,900,000	9,320,000
Shamanism	2,740,000	5,000,000

right next door to a large Wiccan bookstore in a major city. For a sampling of how massive the New Age is on the Internet, I have listed a few of the more common New Age terms and how many times they show up (in quotes) on a Google search on the Internet. It will give you a good idea of what I am talking about.

These figures illustrate beyond doubt how widespread the reach is on the Internet for those who have even the slightest interest in the metaphysical. As more and more people become accustomed to using the Internet, this unlimited access will have a staggering impact on virtually every family in the Western world.

The Secret

In early 2007, the New Age movement got one of its most powerful boosts ever when Oprah Winfrey devoted two whole shows to a book and DVD called *The Secret*. *The Secret* is based on the New Age concept called the *Law of Attraction*. This means whatever you think—you make happen. This includes things like getting sick or accidents that occur or even physical, emotional, or sexual abuse. You brought it on yourself by thinking it first. *The Secret* explains what makes this possible when it says:

> You are God in a physical body. . . . You are all power. . . . You are all intelligence. . . . You are the creator.[26]

Rhonda Byrne, the Australian woman who put the DVD and book together, gives credit in the front of the book to Jerry and Esther Hicks and "the teachings of Abraham."[27] If you believe this is the Abraham spoken of in the Bible, you will be mistaken. This Abraham is described as a large number of spirit guides who collectively go by that name. On the Hicks' website, Abraham is explained:

Abraham, a group of obviously evolved teachers, speak their broader Non-physical perspective through the physical body of Esther [Hicks]. Speaking to our level of comprehension, from their present moment to our now, through a series of loving, allowing, brilliant yet comprehensively simple, recordings in print, in video, and in sound—they guide us to a clear connection with our Inner Being—they guide us to self-upliftment from our total self [god-self].[28]

When Byrne sums up the message of *The Secret* at the end of the DVD and book she is conveying what these "teachers" want the masses turning to this view to know:

No matter who you thought you were, now you know the Truth of Who You Really Are. *You are the master of the Universe.* You are the heir to the kingdom. You are the perfection of Life. And now you know *The Secret.* (emphasis mine)[29]

The Secret came out in 2006, but just since Oprah's promotion of it, sales have soared. As of this writing, over 3.75 million copies of the book are in print, and that number is most likely to grow substantially. One article notes:

"The Secret" dramatically portrays how a number of successful visionaries and motivators have achieved phenomenal results in their lives through the application of the scientific principle called the Law of Attraction. The Law of Attraction simply states that the thoughts we choose to think and the ideas we choose to believe determine the circumstances of our lives, good or bad. By consciously choosing thoughts and beliefs of success, we can program our subconscious minds to attract that success into our lives.[30]

Most of *The Secret's* "visionaries" are major proponents of New Age meditation, such as Jack Canfield (*Chicken Soup for the Soul* creator) who says:

> I attended a meditation retreat that permanently changed my entire life. . . . As you meditate and become more spiritually attuned, you can better discern and recognize the sound of your higher self or the voice of God speaking to you through words, images, and sensations.[31]

I believe it is apparent that with *The Secret* some kind of threshold has been crossed, a flood gate has been opened. Metaphysics is now pouring into many, if not most, families in the Western world through the formats I have outlined in this chapter. Oprah told her viewers, on one of the weeks she featured *The Secret* that this is the message she has been trying to convey to people for twenty years.[32] Even if Oprah and Wayne Dyer were the only ones promoting New Age spirituality, just these two *alone* would be enough to invoke a significant change in our culture. When you add all the other elements such as radio, magazines, movies, etc., almost every person in the Western world has been influenced, either directly or indirectly by New Age concepts.

EIGHT

NEW AGE IN SELF-HELP

FEW would argue that America is riddled with hurting and depressed people. Broken homes, violence, abuse, debt, and crime have affected most people to one degree or another. Drugs, alcohol, and food addictions are also out of control. To deal with these problems, family therapy, personal counseling, and enough self-help teachings through seminars, books, and tapes to last a lifetime have appeared. These huge numbers of needy people have provided a perfect opportunity for the New Age movement that says these souls need to get in touch with their *inner wisdom* in order to heal their troubled lives.

New Age Rehabilitators

Those who teach and implement New Age techniques have permeated the fields of alcohol, drug, and food addiction, as well as family-therapy counseling. One publication referred to these rehabilitators as pioneers on the forefront of the next stage of global and human development.

The New Age program for America's addicted and distraught is remarkably simple in its approach. The idea is to replace substance and other abuses with *consciousness expansion*. To change bad behavior, all they need to do is get people to meditate. This emphasis began to emerge in the late 1980s. It was known to most people as the recovery movement. In many cities you could find whole bookstores devoted entirely to this subject. This widespread appeal motivated me to continue my research of the New Age in earnest. I realized this was a highly effective way to draw in portions of society that would not be attracted to metaphysics otherwise.

One of the prime examples of this effort is the work of author, counselor, and theologian John Bradshaw. He has written five *New York Times* best-sellers: *Bradshaw On: The Family, Healing the Shame That Binds You, Homecoming, Creating Love*, and *Family Secrets*. With his keen insights, Bradshaw has often been referred to as "America's leading personal growth expert."[1] Talk-show host Oprah Winfrey informed her audience that millions are lining up to hear his message. *Newsweek* stated that his seminars were being sold out weeks in advance. Many have called him the leading evangelist of the recovery movement.

Bradshaw is a very articulate and effective speaker. His popularity springs from his ability to make sense of the root causes of personal and family dysfunction. He relates:

> Every addict has a god, be it work, money, booze, cocaine, a lover, a spouse, a child, gambling, nicotine, sex, food, etc. . . . No God ever had a more devoted follower. Addicts literally are ready and willing to give their life for their God.[2]

He says that this is basically a spiritual problem that requires a *spiritual* remedy. For Bradshaw, that remedy is the Ancient Wisdom. He explains the meditation process in the following way:

> *After much practice* you can create a state of
> mindlessness. This state is called the silence. Once
> the silence is created, an unused mental faculty is
> activated. It is a form of intuition. With this faculty
> one can know God directly. Spiritual masters
> present a rather uniform witness on this point.
> They speak of this intuitive knowing variously as
> "untuitive consciousness," or God consciousness, or
> higher consciousness. It is direct union with God.[3]

This "union" is with the classic occult concept of God. If
God is everything and we are part of everything—then we are
God. Bradshaw explains:

> *Each of us in his own way is the universe.* This is what
> all the great spiritual masters have been teaching
> us for centuries. The ego creates separation and
> illusion. Once beyond ego there is no separation.
> We are all one.[4]

To "know" yourself as you really are is a reference to the
all-knowing *inner divinity* that New Agers seek to connect with.
Bradshaw proclaims:

> *The more we are truly ourselves, the more we are truly*
> *Godlike.* To truly be ourselves, we need to accept
> our eternal mission and destiny. This consists in
> manifesting in a fully human way our Godlikeness.[5]

Melody Beattie is a popular author in the field of *co-
dependency*. She has written several best-sellers including *Beyond
Co-Dependency*, *Co-Dependent No More*, and *The Language of Letting
Go*. Although the first two books were non-metaphysical, she
came out of the New Age closet with one called *Co-Dependents'
Guide to the Twelve Steps*.

In the chapter on spiritual awakening she says that to

"connect with God" we need to open our minds to a "higher consciousness" and that we "build a connection to God by building a connection to *ourselves*" *(emphasis* mine).[6]

In the back of this book under a Spiritual Recovery book list, *fifteen* out of the sixteen books listed are hard-core *New* Age books including two that are channeled from a spirit guide.

The common theme of her *comments* in this section is that these books will "change," "alter," and "expand," one's concepts of God and spirituality, "breaking old patterns" and giving one a "new look at life."[7] Ironically, the first book listed is the Bible, which she calls "a favorite source" for those in recovery. Beattie had her own spiritual awakening, not by reading the Bible but by smoking pot. While "high" one day in 1973, she experienced the "power of the Universe" speaking to her, and as a result, she now believes that was her "spiritual awakening." "It transformed me," she said. "It transformed my life."[8]

Just as I expected it would, the recovery movement expanded or rather dissolved into the whole self-help movement. Now, virtually every problem that exists is addressed by New Age writers. The self-help sections of bookstores actually contain more New Age books than the section titled "Metaphysics." Therefore, numerous authors who should be found under "Metaphysics" are always located in self-help. These include Deepak Chopra, Louise Hay, Wayne Dyer, Julia Cameron and M. Scott Peck. Through the avenue of self-help, many people have been introduced to the view that meditation and spirituality are always part of the same package. They always go together.

Women Who Love Too Much by Robin Norwood (a family and child therapist) is a multi-million copy best-seller. My local public library purchased nineteen copies of this book to keep up with the demand. The book deals with relationship addiction, defined by Norwood as when your partner is inappropriate, uncaring, or unavailable—yet you cannot give him up. Norwood's analysis of the problem hits home. She says that women should stop seeing men (especially those who are messed up) as the main source of their happiness and fulfillment. Norwood strongly emphasizes that women should not focus their happiness and well-being on human partners but rather on *spiritual* things. She explains why "spiritual development"[9] is important:

> Without spiritual development, it is nearly impossible to let go of managing and controlling and to believe that all will work out as it is meant to.... Without spiritual development, it is nearly impossible to let go of self-will, and without letting go of self-will you will not be able to take the next step.[10]

In the back of her book under Suggested Reading, Norwood shows the *nature* of "the next step" very clearly. She refers to Catherine Ponders" classic, *The Dynamic Laws of Prosperity*, as "one of my favorite books on metaphysics." The next book on the list is *The Game of Life and How to Play It* by occultist Florence Scovel Shinn. She refers to it as a "masterpiece on metaphysics," and tells her readers, "If you don't have a spiritual practice and wish you did, this book may be a good place to start."[11]

The Art of Living

Not all New Age approaches in this field are geared toward ending dysfunctional behaviors. The other major draw is to enhance an otherwise normal life. They promise, with certain practices and beliefs, you can move from a mundane existence to a radiantly fulfilling one. There are numerous such authors in this genre. One of the more popular and enduring ones is Alexandra Stoddard. She has written twenty-five books on life enhancement, geared mainly toward middle class women. Thus her theme is the *art of living*. Her approach is a skillful blending of the traditional, the practical, and the metaphysical. In her 2006 book *You are Your Choices*, she writes of "an awakening to the divine spirit that exists inside us"[12] and "when we are in a state of higher consciousness . . . quieting our mind, we know things to be true intuitively."[13]

In fact, anyone reading this book would be challenged with the concept that "our consciousness is only half awake if we don't embrace the transcendental and metaphysical."[14]

These topics are overtly religious in nature, yet they are found in self-help sections, not in religious ones. And the most popular New Age figures such as Wayne Dyer and Deepak Chopra are usually featured as self-help. The message is always the same . . . tune into higher consciousness! This approach is more comfortable and has broader appeal than one that is overtly religious, which turns many people off. This is why the self-help arena is one of the more influential manifestations of New Age spirituality.

Another widely known author in this field is Susan Jeffers. Her book, *Feel the Fear and Do It Anyway* has sold two million copies. These sales have given Jeffers the status of the *Queen of Self-Help*. She addresses the issue of self-limiting phobias such as fear of public speaking or fear of romantic commitment. Her answer is to turn to the higher self to solve these dilemmas. I find it noteworthy that Jeffers also uses the term *superconscious* in her book. As I pointed out in the previous chapter, the third Harry Potter book uses that same term for the spiritual realm. For those millions of Harry Potter readers, this correlation could be a catalyst for moving in a mystical direction.

Self-Help Tapes and CDs

Self-help cassette tapes and CDs have become very popular. Through the use of hypnosis, they claim to change unwanted behavior by reprogramming the subconscious mind with subliminal messages that will influence the person toward *the desired* effect. These messages are appealing because they promise to resolve bad habits and develop good ones without pain or effort. This is supposedly accomplished by listening to the sounds of the ocean or soft music while the real message is being slipped to you subliminally (below your conscious awareness level).

The mind boggles at the array of promised benefits listed

within audio cassette catalogs. Virtually every problem one could ever imagine is there, from acne to jet lag. The major themes in these tapes include success, overcoming phobias, health and fitness, erasing bad habits, sports, love, and relationships. According to their catalogs, these tapes have helped thousands with backaches, stress, smoking, weight problems, and more. Although they come across as being strictly non-religious and purely scientific, many of these programs are clearly part of the human potential aspect of the New Age movement. You do not have to look very hard to find the Ancient Wisdom mixed in.

Steven Halpern is widely regarded as the *father* of New Age music. His pieces have a spiritual aspect to them, which is not surprising—many of them are channeled. Once, while meditating amongst the redwoods, he received guidance that there should be music that would "heal."[15] This music is designed to induce a meditative state just by listening to it. When asked if this was possible, he responded:

> There are ways of *stimulating alpha waves*—those brain waves that occur when a person is relaxed—by playing music that resonates with such harmonics. *These harmonics may be engineered right into compositions—such* as in my *Spectrum Suite* or *Crystal Suite*—which trigger the production of alpha." (emphasis mine)[16]

This is what the intention is. In the same interview, he revealed:

> In regard to the field of New Age music, we recognize that it is music *specifically created* to help people *tune in to their Higher Nature.* (emphasis mine).[17]

What is so significant about all this is that he acknowledged: "I've been able to get my music into many hospitals."[18] Consider this reality in light of his following revelation:

For me, a Gold Record is when someone writes and tells me that a tape has touched their heart and opened them to a higher level of awareness and *attunement with their Higher Self.* (emphasis mine)[19]

Hypnosis Practitioners

Practically every practitioner of hypnosis I have come across during my years of research has had a noticeable bent toward metaphysics. Even if it seems unapparent at first, many hypnotherapists engage in such therapies as *past life* regressions, which means that they accept reincarnation as being legitimate. Concerning this link, consider the following case recounted by a young woman:

> I met a woman who was studying for her Ph.D. in psychology and experimenting with past life regression. I volunteered to be one of her subjects, and it was a day that has forever changed my life. During the regression, a "consciousness," which explained itself as a guide, began talking through me to the psychologist. I had the bizarre sensation of being somewhere else, though at the time was vaguely conscious of a conversation taking place. I decided it was the most peculiar experience. My first experience as a medium![20]

Another woman recalled:

> One of my earliest and most powerful hypnotherapy experiences was meeting my inner guide.[21]

Now a hypnotherapist herself, she is doing the same thing for those who come to her for a variety of problems. She states:

> Although meeting my inner guide was a very
> moving experience, I also have the great fortune
> of helping others meet their guides.[22]

While it would be ridiculous to suggest that everyone who gets hypnotized automatically winds up as a channeler, these incidents would explain why so many hypnotherapists are also involved with the Ancient Wisdom. I believe there is a link between the hypnotic state and the meditative state. This relationship between hypnotherapy and New Age beliefs brings to mind the old adage *where there's smoke there's fire.*

A brochure for a method called, Alchemical Hypnotherapy, made the following claims for its effectiveness:

- Addiction recovery
- Healing survivors of childhood abuse and molestation
- Weight management
- Smoking cessation
- Physical illness
- Stress management
- Enhancing creative potential and achieving peak performance
- Solving relationship problems
- Motivation and career success.[23]

But when you read on in the brochure, you find out how these achievements are actually done. A wellness consultant proudly discloses:

> My work has for some time been based on empowering
> my clients. Alchemy empowers my clients in a brand
> new way because of the inner resources that we
> discover during each session. Seeing a client smile or
> cry when they bond with their inner child, *meet their
> guides,* or create a new family experience makes my
> work so rewarding, because I know they are taking
> these *wonderful new friends* home with them for their
> daily life. (emphasis mine)[24]

The Sacred Prostitute

T antra is the name of the ancient Hindu sacred texts that contain certain rituals and secrets. Some deal with taking the energies brought forth in meditation through the chakras and combining them with love-making to enhance sexual experiences.

Once completely off-limits to the masses of humanity, tantra, like all other New Age methodologies, is now starting to gain increasing popularity. A Google search on the Internet shows over 22,000,000 entries for the word *tantra*! This union of sexuality and Eastern spirituality is a perfect example to illustrate just how much the New Age has permeated our society as it has affected even the most intimate areas of people's lives.

The potential to impact a very great number of people, especially men, was brought out in an article by a sex worker who incorporates "Tantric Bodywork" into her services. She paints a very sad portrait of the dynamics of the "enormous sex industry" in which millions of stressed and unhappy men seek out "erotic release" from women who are just as unhappy and stressed as their clients. She observes that there is a "culturally rampant phenomenon that spouses are disconnected from each other."[25]

To remedy this tragic interplay of exploitation, she has turned to *Tantric Union* to give her clients what she feels is not just sex but "union with the divine."[26] After she read a book called *Women of the Light: The New Sacred Prostitute*, she turned her erotic business into a "temple."[27] Of this temple, she says it is:

> . . . dedicated to being a haven of the sacred, a home for the *embodiment of spirit*, filled with altars, sacred objects, plants, art, dreamy sensual music, blissful scents. My space is home to Quan Yin [a Buddhist goddess], crystals blessed by the Entities of John of God [a Brazilian spirit channeler]. (emphasis mine)[28]

Now the "multitudes of men"[29] who come to her get much more than they bargained for. In the past, wives and girlfriends needed only to worry about sexually transmitted diseases from cheating husbands and boyfriends, but now their men may instead bring home *spiritual entities*!

Most readers might think that tantra is something exceedingly obscure that would never attract average people. But the movie industry thinks otherwise. In a 2003 movie, *Hollywood Homicide* (starring Harrison Ford, one of the industry's leading men), viewers were presented with a brief snippet of tantric sex in one scene where fellow police officers opened the locker of Ford's rookie detective partner and out falls a book (which the camera focuses on) about tantra, revealing the side-kick's spiritual/sexual affinities (incidentally, he also teaches yoga in the film).

This again is another indication that the mystical dimension is no longer seen as nonsense or dangerous. The word *occult* used to conjure up images that the typical person would find repellent, but the self-help field has done just the opposite. Now the idea of mystical powers is seen as something that can actually enhance your life and remedy your various maladies. In essence, the wide spread popularity of the New Age/self-help field has made mysticism respectable.

NINE

NEW AGE IN RELIGION

ONE of the main reasons many Christian pastors fail to take the New Age movement seriously is because they are not adept at effectively measuring its real strength. They are accustomed to assessing the prestige and influence of a spiritual movement by its number of churches, attendance records, or television and radio programs. Since they do not see New Age churches on every corner, they tend to discount any cause for alarm.

However, just as business, health care, education, counseling, and other areas of society are being influenced by those who have had transformation experiences, so is American religion. This influence has become so widespread that most mainstream denominations are playing a role in spreading New Age consciousness. Many people would be quite surprised to find that meditation has made its way into both Catholic and Protestant churches on a large scale. Although some would argue that it is not New Age meditation but rather a form of legitimate prayer, evidence proves this is not the case.

Upon close examination, the methods used (mantra, breathing) are *identical* to New Age techniques. Only the connotation is changed. Countless times I have come across such terms as *holistic spirituality* or *combining the mystical traditions of both East and West*. Frequently, the Hindu or Buddhist source of these *spiritual exercises* will be proclaimed openly.

Centering Prayer

In the book, *Finding Grace at the Center*, which was written by several proponents of centering prayer,* the following statements are made:

> We should not hesitate to take the fruit of the age-old wisdom of the East and "capture" it for Christ. Indeed, those of us who are in ministry should make the necessary effort to acquaint ourselves with as many of these Eastern techniques as possible.[1]

> Many Christians who take their prayer life seriously have been greatly helped by Yoga, Zen, TM, and similar practices, especially where they have been initiated by reliable teachers and have a solidly developed Christian faith to give inner form and meaning to the resulting experiences.[2]

In view of this, it is no wonder that I encountered a woman in a Christian bookstore who enthusiastically told me that in her church "we use a *mantra* to get in touch with God."

Being touted as an *ancient prayer* form, the centering prayer employs a mantra (called the *prayer word*) that allows one to empty the mind by chanting *Jesus, God,* or *love* rather than *om* or *Krishna*.

Centering prayer groups are flourishing in mainstream religious bodies today. Many times those who embrace these practices

*To read more about centering prayer and the contemplative prayer movement, read *A Time of Departing*, 2nd ed., 2006, Lighthouse Trails Publishing.

are the most active and creative people in the congregation. They are seen by many as bringing a new vitality to the church.

Basil Pennington relates in his book, *Centering Prayer*, how he shared this method with someone from another religious background. For those who doubt that this form of prayer should be seen as New Age, I recommend they consider the following account:

> I presented the Centering Prayer in my usual way, wondering what chords of response this call to faith and love might be striking in the Hindu monk. We soon entered into the prayer and enjoyed that beautiful fullness of silence. As we came out of the experience I shot a concerned glance in the direction of our Eastern friend. He had—or, I could almost say, was—a most beautiful smile, a deep, radiant expression of peaceful joy. Gently he gave his witness: "This has been the most beautiful experience I have ever had." This was for me on many levels a very affirming experience.[3]

Another widely popular book on this is *Sadhana: A Way To God* by Jesuit priest, Anthony de Mello. Sadhana, according to de Mello, means "spiritual exercises."[4] This book is very open in its acknowledgment of Eastern mysticism as an enrichment to Christian spirituality. De Mello lets his readers know at the very beginning just where he is coming from:

> A Jesuit friend once told me that he approached a Hindu guru for initiation in the art of prayer. The guru said to him, "*Concentrate on your breathing.*" My friend proceeded to do just that for about five minutes. Then the guru said, "*The air you breathe is God. You are breathing God in and out. Become aware of that, and stay with that awareness.*"[5]

The following statement by de Mello could have been made

by *any* New Ager: "I want you now to discover the revelation that silence brings."[6]

Silence, of course, is the blank mind that you have been reading about. This word is used as a buzz word by many in metaphysics. When a person is in this state, he is *open* to the *Universe*.

De Mello explains what it is like to experience "silence,"[7] which is the logical progression in the *Sadhana* process—an altered state of consciousness:

> There will be moments when the stillness of the *blank* will be so powerful that it will make all exercise and all effort on your part impossible. In such moments it is no longer you who goes in quest of stillness. It is stillness that *takes possession of you* and *overwhelms you*. When this happens, you may safely, and profitably, let go of all effort (which has become impossible, anyway) and surrender to this overpowering stillness within you. (emphasis mine)[8]

This great "stillness" or silence is termed in Hinduism Samadhi, which is a deep mystical state induced by focus on something repetitive. Catholic Jesuit priest William Johnson actually makes the case that this state is the same as its Eastern equivalent when he informs us that:

> The twentieth century, which has seen so many revolutions, is now witnessing the rise of a new mysticism within Christianity. . . . For the new mysticism has learned much from the great religions of Asia. It has felt the impact of yoga and Zen and the monasticism of Tibet. It pays attention to posture and breathing; it knows about the music of the mantra and the silence of samadhi.[9]

De Mello's book, *Sadhana*, has had an enormous impact on both clergy and laity. One source reveals:

This book has come to be recognized universally as a masterpiece in the art of teaching people how to pray. After its first publication in 1979, it ranked among the top U.S. Catholic best sellers for many years. Just to read it is a captivating and challenging experience. More than 20 translations have been published. Now all over the world this classic text has been acclaimed as the best how-to-do-it book on prayer available in any language. Sadhana is perhaps the best book available today in English for Christians on how to pray, meditate, and contemplate.[10]

It has been highly praised by church leaders and theologians. The back cover of the book includes the following statement made by a leading church figure:

[P]erhaps the best book available today in English for Christians on how to pray, meditate, and contemplate.[11]

It is often used as a textbook to teach people how to pray. Catholic parishes, nursing facilities, hospitals, retirement centers, and religious communities are using it on a regular basis.

I'm sure many of these people would be surprised if they learned what the Hindu connotation of *Sadhana* meant. A dictionary on Hinduism reveals the following:

Siddhis [psychic powers] are also considered to be the direct or indirect result of a quest for enlightenment or knowledge. The pursuit of any method for attaining to such knowledge is termed *sadhana*, 'gaining;' the person practicing sadhana is called a *sadhaka* (fem. *sadhika)*, and the successful sadhaka is a *sadhu*. Since siddhis are magical in character, the terms *sadhana* and *sadhu* are also frequently used for sorcery and sorcerer respectively.[12]

The literal meaning for *Sadhana: A Way to God,* according to this definition, would then be *Sorcery: A Way to God!*

Meditation is also being taught within the parochial school systems, generally at the high school and college levels. Students at Catholic schools have revealed to me that mantra meditation is part of their curriculum and that these classes are led by priests. One Catholic high school textbook titled *Your Faith and You: A Synthesis of Catholic Belief* reveals the following in the chapter titled "Prayer, Seeking Union With God":

> Numerous Catholic retreat houses offer "Yoga retreats" or teach Zen meditation methods. But these techniques are totally removed [borrowed] from the Buddhist or Hindu faiths. They are often used by Christians to help them develop a conscious faith relationship with Christ in prayer. Likewise, the Buddhist or Hindu uses these same techniques to enter into a deeper union with God as his own religion has taught him to believe in him.[13]

I wonder how it is possible that Christians can use the same techniques that Buddhists and Hindus use to reach their gods without, in fact, *reaching their gods.*

Metaphysical meditation remains exactly the same no matter what name you tag on it. Changing the mantras does not make it *Christian.*

What is happening is that this melding of meditative practices is producing some major changes in mainstream Christianity. Many are being taught that centering prayer is the most direct route to God. This in turn, is producing what one writer terms "full Christianity."[14] He explains:

> Indeed today catholics practice Zen meditation. There are Christian-Hindu monasteries in India. And Fr. Raimundo Panikkar has suggested that

Indian philosophy might prove a better base for Christian theology than Aristotle.

Thomas Merton predicted that the twenty-first century would belong to two things: Christianity and Zen. Today these great traditions as well as others are meeting one another in a spirit of humble inquiry. Perhaps it is just this coming together of our world traditions that will provide the spiritual impetus needed to usher in a new age of the Spirit.[15]

Filling the Vacuum

Why are the mainstream denominations so open to meditative and holistic practices? A professor of theology at a United Methodist college gave this explanation:

A spiritual vacuum exists in organized religion that might be filled by theologies that draw—for better or worse—from what is called parapsychology, paranormal studies, psychic phenomena and, somewhat pejoratively, the "New Age" movement.[16]

New Agers have become very much aware of this "spiritual vacuum" and have directed their efforts toward filling it. Metaphysical leader James Fadiman makes the following observation:

The traditional religious world is just beginning to make changes, but it's a slow process—denomination by denomination. When religious institutions begin to lose members year after year, they eventually become aware that they're not meeting people's needs. Before long they're scurrying around looking for innovative programs and improvements.[17]

Even atheists have observed this trend. Science-fiction writer Richard E. Geis comments in his personal journal that:

> The mainstream Christians are lip-service religions
> in the main, convenience religions, social religions,
> and they are the ones most subject to erosion and
> defections and infiltration and subversion. A large
> and successful effort seems to have been made by
> the occultists' New Age planners to dilute and alter
> the message of most of the mainstream Christian
> religions.[18]

This is made evident by a quote which appeared in a newspaper interview with the owner of a New Age bookstore. She reveals:

> A lot of people come in who are very Christian.
> They are looking, by whatever means, to move closer
> to God on an individual basis.[19]

This shows that a great number of people who consider themselves to be Christians have a rather dull and dreary attitude toward their faith. They are looking for something to fill the void.

One of the foremost individuals who has attempted to fill this void with the New Age is Marcus Borg, professor and author of many widely read books. In one of them, *The God We Never Knew*, he lays out very concisely how he went from being a traditional Christian to a "mature" Christian. He relates:

> I learned from my professors and the readings they
> assigned that Jesus almost certainly was not born
> of a virgin, did not think of himself as the Son of
> God, and did not see his purpose as dying for the
> sins of the world. . . . By the time I was thirty, like
> Humpty Dumpty, my childhood faith had fallen
> into pieces. My life since has led to a quite different
> understanding of what the Christian tradition says
> about God.[20]

Like multitudes of liberal Christians who believe as he does, Borg turned to mysticism to fill the spiritual vacuum that his way of thinking inevitably leads to. Borg reveals:

> I learned about the use of mantras as a means of giving the mind something to focus and refocus on as it sinks into silence.[21]

This is a recurring theme in all his books, including his very influential book, *The Heart of Christianity*. Even though Marcus Borg would certainly not call himself a New Ager, his practices and views on God would be in line with traditional New Age thought (i.e., God is in everything and each person is a receptacle of the Divine, which is accessed through meditation).

Borg is a key example of what I am trying to convey in this chapter. He is not some Hindu guru or counter-culture type personality. He represents the mainstream for millions of people in liberal churches. But his spiritual platform is pure New Age as he makes clear when he expounds:

> The sacred is not "somewhere else" spatially distant from us. Rather, we live within God . . . God has always been in relationship to us, journeying with us, and yearning to be known by us. Yet we commonly do not know this or experience this. . . . We commonly do not *perceive the world of Spirit*. (emphasis mine)[22]

This perception is, of course, as I have shown earlier, the outcome of mantra-induced silence.

The following is another barometer of Christian tolerance to New Age ideas. The late psychologist M. Scott Peck wrote a phenomenal best seller on psychology and spiritual growth titled *The Road Less Traveled*. The book contains insights and suggestions for dealing with life's problems, which is why it has generated the interest it has. But the book also incorporates the central theme of the Ancient Wisdom:

God wants us to become himself (or Herself or Itself). We are growing toward godhood. God is the goal of evolution. It is God who is the source of the evolutionary force and God who is the destination. This is what we mean when we say that He is the Alpha and the Omega, the beginning and the end.. . .
It is one thing to believe in a nice old God who will take good care of us from a lofty position of power which we ourselves could never begin to attain. It is quite another to believe in a God who has it in mind for us precisely that we should attain His position, His power, His wisdom, His identity.[23]

Madame Blavatsky and Alice Bailey could not have said it any better. Peck revealed where he was coming from when he said, "But (The Road) is a sound New Age book, not a flaky one."[24] This book, which was on the New York Times best seller list for over 400 weeks, has been incredibly popular in Christian circles for years. Peck himself said the book sells best in the Bible Belt.

Kabbalah

When most people hear the term New Age, what comes to their minds is a perception of something on the lunatic fringe of society. Hardly anyone would link that term with an established, respectable religion. But as you are hopefully learning, this is not the case anymore. Now even Judaism is becoming part of the New Age trend. A formerly obscure practice known as the Kabbalah (Jewish mysticism) is making inroads into Judaism in much the same way centering prayer is into Christianity.

Kabbalistic Jews practice New Age style meditation and have powerful experiences of energies called sephirot that engulf their bodies. God is referred to as Ein Sof or Limitless Light. It is essentially the same experiences and practices as other forms of New Age mysticism, only within a Jewish context.

An entire publishing house has sprung up to feed the interest in Kabbalah. Its name, Jewish Lights, reflects the view of New Age spirituality that one must become enlightened to make the Aquarian Age a reality.

Another major force in Judaism for the Kabbalah is Rabbi Philip Berg with his numerous books on the subject and dozens of Kabbalah Centres around the world, bringing the "once-secret ancient wisdom of Kabbalah to the public."[25] Rabbi Berg believes that "the fate of the world rested on everyone having access to Kabbalah."[26] The Kabbalah Centre has one hundred instructors who teach the Kabbalah over the phone to students around the world, and its website receives over 100,000 visitors a week.

One author in particular who embodies this movement within Judaism is Melinda Ribner. She was right on the money when she named her book *New Age Judaism: Ancient Wisdom for the Modern World*. Like a Jewish version of Wayne Dyer, she explains:

> Judaism offers a variety of meditation techniques to increase God-awareness. Meditation is an important practice of the New Age as well because it transforms our consciousness in a quick and powerful way. Over the years, I have witnessed the most miraculous transformations of my students through the practice of meditation.[27]

As with Marcus Borg, many people in respectable religious circles no longer view this activity with suspicion or amusement. What once was thought to be wacky is now the way to know God deeply. Ribner explains:

> Judaism is undergoing an exciting renaissance today. The House of Israel is once again being rebuilt. There is increasing vitality in all branches of Judaism . . . Religious organizations are slowly

responding to the pressure put upon them to bring forth mystical teachings. I have seen several orthodox Jewish organizations begin to offer classes in kabbalah when only last year they spoke out vehemently against the study of kabbalah. Even rabbis in the Reform movement of Judaism are teaching kabbalah.[28]

A Global Religion

What is happening to mainstream Christianity is the same thing that is happening to business, health, education, counseling, and other areas of society. Christendom is being cultivated for a role in the New Age. The entity, Raphael, explains this very clearly in the *Starseed Transmissions:*

> We work with all who are vibrationally sympathetic; simple and sincere people who feel our spirit moving, but for the most part, *only within the context of their current belief system.* (emphasis mine)[29]

He is saying that they "work," or interact, with people who open their minds to them in a way that fits in with the person's *current beliefs.* In the context of Christianity this means that those meditating will think that they have contacted God, when in reality they have connected up with Raphael's kind (who are more than willing to impersonate whomever the person wishes to reach so long as they can link with them).

This ultimately points to a global religion based on meditation and mystical experience. New Age writer David Spangler explains it the following way:

> There will be several religious and spiritual disciplines as there are today, each serving different sensibilities and affinities, each enriched by and enriching the particular cultural soil in which it is rooted. However,

there will also be a *planetary spirituality* that will celebrate the sacredness of the whole of humanity in appropriate festivals, rituals, and sacraments. There will be a more widespread understanding and experience of the holistic nature of reality, resulting in a shared outlook that today would be called mystical. Mysticism has always overflowed the bounds of particular religious traditions, and in the new world this would be even more true.[30]

The rise of centering prayer is causing many churches to become *agents of transformation*. Those who practice it tend to embrace this one-world-religion idea. One of the main proponents of centering prayer had this revelation:

It is my sense, from having meditated with persons from many different traditions, that *in the silence we experience a deep unity*. When we go beyond the portals of the rational mind into the experience, there is only one God to be experienced. . . . I think it has been the common experience of all persons of good will that when we sit together Centering we experience *a solidarity* that seems to *cut through all our philosophical and theological differences*. (emphasis mine)[31]

In this context, we may compare all the world's religions to a dairy herd. Each cow may look different on the outside, but the milk would all be the same. The different religious groups would maintain their own separate identities, but a universal spiritual practice would bind them together—not so much a one-world church as a one-world spirituality.

Episcopal priest and New Age leader Matthew Fox explains what he calls "deep ecumenism":

Without mysticism there will be no "deep ecumenism," no unleashing of the power of wisdom

from all the world's religious traditions. Without
this I am convinced there will never be global peace
or justice since the human race needs spiritual
depths and disciplines, celebrations and rituals, to
awaken its better selves. The promise of ecumenism,
the coming together of religions, has been thwarted
because world religions have not been relating at
the level of mysticism.[32]

Fox believes that all world religions will eventually be bound
together by the "Cosmic Christ"[33] principle, which is another
term for the higher self.

As incredible as this may sound, it appears to be happening now.
The New Age is embedded in American religious culture far deeper
and broader than many people imagine. If your concept of the New
Age is simply astrology, tarot cards, or reincarnation, then you could
easily miss the *real* New Age as it pulses through the religious current.
If mystical prayer continues its advance, then we could one day see,
perhaps sooner than we expect, many Christian churches becoming
conduits of New Age thought to their membership.

Is God Graffiti?

Sue Monk Kidd is a best selling novel writer. Her book, *The
Secret Life of Bees* has sold over four million copies, mainly to
women. At one time a Southern Baptist Sunday school teacher,
she became attracted to centering prayer as a way to know God
more deeply. Today, she is the Writer in Residence of the Sophia
Institute, which is devoted to "foster[ing] the emergence of the
sacred feminine" (i.e., the Divine feminine).[34]

Monk Kidd now adheres to what New Agers teach, that
this mystical force (called *God* or *Divinity*) is in all things,
nothing excluded:

Deity means that divinity will no longer be only
heavenly . . . It will also be right here, right now, in

me, in the earth, in this river, in *excrement and roses
alike.* (emphasis mine) [35]

She reiterates this in her 2006 book, *First Light,* in which
she writes:

> If I am intent on centering my life in the presence
> of God, then I must understand what I believe
> about where this presence can be found . . . God
> became the steam of my soup, the uprooted tree,
> the graffiti on the building, the rust on the fence. [36]

But what if the graffiti is gang graffiti about killing members
of a rival gang or even worse, what if the graffiti is cursing God
with vile language?

Well, Monk Kidd would *still* say that the graffiti is God.

Why?

It is because New Agers believe God is not a being but Being
itself. In other words, there is nothing that is not God. This is the
decision that the world is now facing—is God a personal being
or is God *the Universe* and all that it entails? It is this vital question that we will explore in the following chapters of this book.

TEN

IS THE NEW AGE WRONG?

IN the first nine chapters of this book, we examined the origin, essence, and thrust of metaphysics today. I do not agree with the view that the New Age is the path to the Golden Age of global peace and harmony.

But after 22 years of research, I fully understand why so many people *have* embraced metaphysics and why they seek transformation for humanity as a whole. By and large, they have rejected orthodox (old paradigm) Christianity as being unacceptable, but still want to retain spiritual meaning and a utopian vision in their lives. In addition, they see metaphysics as helpful towards improving the quality of their daily lives, whether it be better health, more loving relationships, inner peace, or guidance for success and prosperity. They would think it the height of ignorance and folly to condemn such seemingly wonderful ways to better the human condition.

Many would reject a challenge of New Age consciousness from a Christian viewpoint as being the result of misinformation. It is widely believed in New Age circles that Jesus Christ was Himself a metaphysician of great stature. They quote verses where Jesus proclaims: "The kingdom of God is within you" (Luke 17:21)—meaning a reference to the higher self, "Be still and know that I am God" (Psalm 46:10)—a reference, they say, to meditation, and "Greater works than these shall he do" (John 14:12)—meaning New Agers can have His powers. As far out as this may sound to many Christian readers, New Age adherents are quite sincere in this belief. They firmly argue that reincarnation was originally in the Bible but was taken out at the Council of Nicea so that church and state could better control the common people by fear. Although there are still plenty of skeptics and critics, these beliefs are becoming less offensive and more acceptable all the time.

One of the most common New Age attitudes is that there are *many* paths to God and that it is wrong to judge or condemn another person's path because not all people are suited for the same one. New Agers teach that each person should find the path best suited for himself.

To Judge or Not Be Judged

There are two questions to be answered here: Is it right to judge? And do all paths lead to God? Jesus Christ foretold in Matthew 7:22-23:

> Many will say to me in that day, "Lord, Lord, have we not prophesied in thy name? and in thy name have cast out devils? and in thy name done many wonderful works?" And then will I profess unto them, "I never knew you: depart from me, ye that work iniquity."

I find it most interesting that people who were doing "many wonderful works" or miraculous works in *His* name were, in reality, working "iniquity" or evil. This leads me to believe that a great deception is occurring.

These verses also tell me that all paths *do not* lead to God and, because they do not, one had better judge which path is correct. Many people, of course, counter with, "Judge not, that ye be not judged." However, taken in context, this verse (Matthew 7:1), is talking about hypocrisy in human behavior and not about withholding critical examination of spiritual teachings. Galatians 1:8 bears out the necessity to *evaluate* spiritual teaching with proper discernment. Paul warns:

> But though we, or an angel from heaven, *preach any other gospel* unto you than that which we have preached unto you, let him be accursed. (emphasis mine)

And II John 1:9-11 says:

> Whosoever transgresseth, and abideth not in the doctrine of Christ, *hath not God.* He that abideth in the *doctrine* of Christ, he *hath both the Father and the Son.* If there come any unto you, and bring not this doctrine, receive him not into your house, neither bid him God speed: For he that biddeth him God speed is partaker of his evil deeds. (emphasis mine)

And again in Ephesians 5:11, "...have no fellowship with the unfruitful works of darkness, but rather *reprove them*" (emphasis mine).

How may we reprove something if we don't determine whether or not it fits the bill of "unfruitful works?" In II Timothy 3:16-17, we read:

> All scripture is given by inspiration of God, and is profitable for doctrine, *for reproof, for correction,* for instruction in righteousness: That the man of God may be perfect [complete], thoroughly furnished [fully equipped] unto all good works. (emphasis mine)

Familiar Spirits

Noticing the New Age propensity for also quoting Bible verses to support the claims of metaphysics, I have focused on the obvious *conflict* between the Ancient Wisdom and the God of the Bible that runs from Genesis through Revelation. The continuity of this apparent contrast is undeniable to the point that any New Ager would have to acknowledge that it exists. This contrast and objection is the foundation for any logical Christian opposition to metaphysics. Notice the list of metaphysical arts in Deuteronomy 18:9-12:

> When thou art come into the land which the Lord thy God giveth thee, thou shalt not learn to do after the *abominations of those nations*. There shall not be found among you any one that maketh his son or his daughter to pass through the fire, or that useth divination [a psychic, or an observer of times, meaning festivals connected to nature worship], or an enchanter [one who manipulates people by occult power], or a witch [one who uses occult power]. Or a charmer [hypnotist], or a *consulter with familiar spirits* [one who receives advice or knowledge from a spirit], or a wizard [one who uses a spirit to do his will], or a necromancer [one who believes he is contacting the dead]. For all that do these things are an abomination unto the Lord: and because of these abominations the Lord thy God doth drive them out from before thee. (emphasis mine)

The word abomination in verse 12 means "abhorrent" or "disgusting." Please note the reference to *familiar spirits* in the following verses from Leviticus. This term is found throughout the Old Testament and has a negative connotation:

> And the soul that turneth after such as have *familiar spirits*, and after wizards, to go a whoring after them,

> I will even set my face against that soul, and will
> cut him off from among his people. (Leviticus 20:6,
> emphasis mine)

An example of this is a book called *Creative Visualization* by Shakti Gawain, which could be called one of the *bibles* of the New Age movement (over three million copies have been sold in the US and translated into 25 languages). Gawain explains the basic process of visualization. First comes "relaxing into a deep, quiet meditative state of mind,"[1] which is to be done every morning and afternoon. This opens the "channel" for "higher wisdom and guidance to come to you."[2] Gawain then describes the nature of this *guidance*:

> The inner guide is known by many different names,
> such as your counselor, spirit guide, imaginary
> friend, or master. It is a higher part of yourself,
> which can come to you in many different forms,
> but usually comes in the form of a person or being
> whom you can talk to and relate to as a wise and
> loving friend.[3]

> Your guide is there for you to call on anytime you
> need or want extra guidance, wisdom, knowledge,
> support, creative inspiration, love or companionship.
> Many people who have established a relationship
> with their guide meet them every day in their
> meditation.[4]

What Shakti Gawain is talking about is the same thing spoken of in Deuteronomy 18–*familiar spirits*. The so-called higher self is nothing more than a familiar spirit out to manipulate those people who open themselves to it. It has been common in Christian circles to speak of them as demons. The word demon comes from the Greek term *deamonion*, which literally means *spirit guide*. Familiar spirits make contact while the person's mind is in neutral and try to establish a strong connection; the result is control of the person by the spirit. The core of New Age spirituality is that the higher self (i.e., familiar spirit) is supposed to be the guiding principle in every area of one's life—period!

That is why in Ephesians 6:12, the apostle Paul warns us:

> For we wrestle not against *flesh and blood*, but against principalities, against powers, against the rulers of the darkness of this world, against spiritual wickedness in high places. (emphasis mine)

He is saying that there are non-human powers (forces) that are in opposition to God. The nature of this is apparent to anyone who takes a close look at metaphysics with this verse in mind. After a certain point, influence and guidance from the familiar spirit progresses to outright possession. This, I believe, is the kundalini effect. One New Age proponent explains it the following way:

> Before, kundalini had seemed like a fable to me, fascinating and appealing, but as improbable in its way as God talking to Moses through a burning bush or Jesus raising the dead. But now I was sometimes aware, toward the end of the third stage of Dynamic Meditation, of something moving as elusively as neon up my spine, flashing like lightning in my limbs. . . . When, in the fifth and final stage, I danced, I now sensed myself moved by a force more powerful, more inventive, than any I could consciously summon.[5]

I believe that Raphael and Alice Bailey's "Tibetan" are familiar spirits. I also believe they are revealing their *plan of operation* in their writings. The intent of these beings can be seen by what the following metaphysical practitioners convey:

It is all there—just look for it. Seek the immortal, eternal Spirit that dwells within you—the "I am presence," containing all that was, is, or ever shall be. . . . The whole of life will become more meaningful as you live from the center within. Remember that you are Gods in the Making.[6]

It is not necessary to "have faith" in any power outside of yourself.[7]

The Angel of Light

W ho do you think would want you to believe something like that? Who would want you to believe that God does not exist *outside of yourself*–that you don't need to have faith in anything *external*. New Age writer/philosopher David Spangler reveals *who* in his book *Reflections on the Christ* when he writes:

> Some being has to take these energies into his consciousness and substance and channel them as it were to those other beings who must receive them, in this case humanity. The being who chose to embody these energies and to be in essence the angel of man's inner evolution is the being we know as Lucifer.[8]

He lays out the entire program behind the New Age movement in the following explanation:

> He [Lucifer] comes to make us aware of our power within, to draw to ourselves experience. He comes to make us aware of the power of creative manifestation which we wield.

> When you are working with the laws of manifestation you are in essence manifesting a Luciferic principle.[9]

Even if Spangler had not written these words, the link between Lucifer and the New Age movement would still be evident to Christians from reading II Corinthians 11:13-15:

> For such are false apostles, deceitful workers, transforming themselves into the apostles of Christ. And no marvel; for *Satan himself is transformed into an angel of light.* Therefore it is no great thing if his ministers also be transformed as the *ministers of righteousness;* whose end shall be according to their works. (emphasis mine)

For this deception to be effective, he would have to come as an "angel of light." To judge a belief system as being satanic, one should compare how close it comes to Satan's own statements about himself. God is asking him, "How art thou fallen from heaven, O Lucifer, son of the morning! How art thou cut down to the ground, which didst weaken the nations!" (Isaiah. 14:12). Then He reminds Satan of his own words when he challenged God:

> For thou [Satan] hast said in thine heart, "I will ascend into heaven, I will exalt my throne above the stars of God: I will sit also upon the mount of the congregation, in the sides of the north: I will ascend above the heights of the clouds; *I will be like the most High.*" (Isaiah 14:13-14, emphasis added)

Then later, when Satan deceived Eve in the Garden, he said:

> For God doth know that in the day ye eat thereof, then your eyes shall be opened, and *ye shall be as gods,* knowing good and evil. (Genesis 3:5, emphasis mine)

Without a doubt, the New Age movement *fits that bill.*

The "Wiles" of Satan

Ephesians 6:11 warns: "Put on the whole armour of God, that ye may be able to stand against the *wiles* of the devil" (emphasis mine).

The word *wiles* in this verse translates *ingenious trap* or *snare*. In order for a trap to be effective, proper bait is needed—something that is alluring, that looks and feels valid. For example, let's take the case of Reiki. The average Reiki practitioner would think it outrageous and ridiculous that someone would even *suggest* that Reiki is linked to Satan. One Reiki practitioner offered this comment on the positive nature of Reiki:

> During a Reiki treatment, you can expect to feel any number of sensations; warmth, coolness, tingling, deep relaxation, or at times you may not feel anything discernible. Sessions usually last one hour, and afterward you will feel calm and relaxed. You will sleep better and have a general sense of well-being.[10]

Does this sound like something that is satanic? Most people would not only say no but would feel that something of this nature probably would have to come from God.

In *The Reiki Factor*, Reiki master Barbara Ray says:

> Reiki has reemerged as a transformative tool for energy balancing, for natural healing, for wholing, and for creating peace, joy, love, and, ultimately, for achieving higher consciousness and enlightenment.[11]

Enlightenment is the same as self-realization, especially in the context of a metaphysical practice. When a Christian hears someone claim to be God, he immediately should recognize the pronouncements of Satan, "Ye shall be as gods" (Genesis 3:5) and "I will be like the most High" (Isaiah 14:14). Hear this closely. He said, I will be *like* the most High (God) . . . *I will be like God.*

In view of this, the only logical conclusion is that the power behind Reiki is *satanic*. The key is not to think in terms of how the popular culture sees Satan, but rather how the inspired writers of the Bible portrayed Satan—a master deceiver and counterfeiter of the truth. He is one who comes as "an angel of light" (II Corinthians 11:14) to offer mankind *godhood* (you are divine and the master of your own destiny).

The sad thing about all this is that these experiences are so real and convincing. People experiencing the superconscious testify that deep meditative states are incomparably beautiful and rapturous. They experience intense light flooding them, and have a sense of omnipotent power and infinite wisdom. In this timeless state, they experience an ecstasy compared to nothing they have ever known before. They feel a sense of unity with all of life and are convinced of their own immortality. Such experiences keep them returning for more. One is not going to *believe* he or she is God if one doesn't *feel* like God.

The late New Age leader Peter Caddy related an incident in which a group of Christians confronted him and tried, as he put it, *to save my soul.* He told them to come back and talk to him when they've had the same wonderful mystical experiences he has had. The point he was trying to make was that these *naive* Christians had no idea what the metaphysical life is all about and if they did, they would want what *he* had rather than trying to convert him to *their* way of thinking.

Feelings such as this are common in New Age circles and have hooked many over the past twenty years. They feel something this great *has* to be of God. A similar account is related in Acts 8:9-11:

> But there was a certain man, called Simon, which beforetime in the same city used sorcery, and bewitched the people of Samaria, giving out that himself was some great one: To whom they all gave heed, from the least to the greatest, saying, This man is the *great power of God*. And to him they had

> regard, because that of long time he had bewitched
> them with sorceries. (emphasis mine)

In the Greek, the word *bewitched* means *to amaze* or astound. *Sorcery* means using the power of familiar spirits. What this man was doing had to have appeared good, otherwise the people would not have felt that "this man is the great power of God." The truth of the matter is, he wasn't of God, it just appeared that way.

In light of all this, it is easy to see why the coming of the Christian Gospel to Ephesus, that bastion of the Ancient Wisdom, had such a dramatic effect:

> And many that believed came, and confessed, and shewed their deeds. Many of them also which used *curious arts* brought their books together, and burned them before all men: and they counted the price of them, and found it fifty thousand pieces of silver. So mightily grew the word of God and prevailed. (Acts 19:18-19, emphasis mine)

The word *curious* is translated from a Greek word meaning *magical*. The magical or metaphysical arts went out the door when the Gospel of Christ came in. The two were not only *incompatible*, but *totally opposite* as the following account reveals:

> And when they were at Salamis, they preached the word of God in the synagogues of the Jews: and they had also John to their minister. And when they had gone through the isle unto Paphos, they found a certain *sorcerer, a false prophet,* a Jew, whose name was Barjesus: Which was with the deputy of the country, Sergius Paulus, a prudent man; who called for Barnabas and Saul, and desired to hear the word of God. But Elymas the sorcerer (for so is his name by interpretation) withstood them, seeking to *turn away the deputy from the*

faith. Then Saul, (who also is called Paul,) filled with
the Holy Ghost, set his eyes on him, And said, O full
of all *subtilty* and all *mischief* thou *child of the devil*, thou
enemy of all righteousness, wilt thou not cease to *pervert
the right ways of the Lord?* (Acts 13:5-10, emphasis mine)

A Distinct Division

If you feel (as many New Agers do) that Jesus' real teachings
were suppressed and distorted, then consider this: Jesus was a good
Jew who strictly adhered to what we now call the Old Testament.
In the Old Testament, as we have seen, contact with familiar spirits
(spirit guides) was strictly forbidden. King Saul is a prime example
of what happened to those who ignored this taboo:

> So Saul died for his transgression which he
> committed against the Lord, even against the *word
> of the LORD, which he kept not,* and also for asking
> counsel of *one that had a familiar spirit,* to inquire
> of it; And inquired not of the Lord: therefore He
> slew him, and turned the kingdom unto David the
> son of Jesse. (I Chronicles 10:13-14, emphasis mine)

Also in Judaism, there was a distinct division between God
and man as the following verses indicate:

> Ye are my witnesses, saith the Lord, and my servant
> whom I have chosen: that ye may know and believe
> me, and understand that I am He: *before me there was
> no God formed, neither shall there be after me. I, even I,
> am the Lord; and beside me there is no saviour.* I have
> declared, and have saved, and I have shewed, when
> there was no strange god among you: therefore ye
> are my witnesses, saith the Lord, that I am God.
> (Isaiah 43:10-12. emphasis mine)

Thus saith the Lord, thy redeemer, and He that

> formed thee from the womb, I am the Lord that
> maketh all things; that stretcheth forth the heavens
> *alone*; that spreadeth abroad the earth *by myself*.
> (Isaiah 44:24, emphasis mine)

In view of this, Jesus *could not* have been a purveyor of the Ancient Wisdom and a devout Jew as well. In the Jewish religion there is *one* Creator/Sustainer and man is *not* Him. He *created* man to worship and give glory to Him. This view remains the basis for the Christian view of God.

Jesus' claim to divinity was based on His Messiahship, a uniquely *Jewish* concept, *not* compatible with the Ancient Wisdom teachings of human divinity. He told the Samaritan woman "salvation is of the Jews" (John 4:22).

To those who have embraced metaphysics as the truth of the universe and the way of salvation, let me say this: I know you are sincere. I know metaphysics makes you feel good about yourself. I know you have rejected *old-paradigm* Christianity as unsuitable. But please give serious consideration to Jeremiah 10:6,11:

> Forasmuch as there is *none like unto thee, O Lord;* thou
> art great, and thy name is great in might. Thus shall ye
> say unto them, the gods that *have not made the heavens
> and the earth,* even they *shall perish from the earth,* and
> from under these heavens. (emphasis mine)

The Folly of the Ages

In II Corinthians 1:9, the apostle Paul says:

> But we had the sentence of death in ourselves, that
> we should not trust in ourselves, but in God which
> raiseth the dead.

The verse does not say we should trust in ourselves who are God—it says we should *not* trust in ourselves but *trust in God*.

God is a personal Being, not the Universe, not a spirit guide, and most certainly *not* humanity.

The reason the New Age is wrong is that it takes devotion, trust, and glory *away* from the One who created us and gives it to man and the rebellious familiar spirits who deceive man into self-glorification. An analogy of this would be that of an artist's canvas or paint—rather than the artist taking credit for the painting, the canvas or paint takes the credit.

That is why the Gentile nations were separated from the true God. They were the metaphysicians of old (the Mystery Schools) "who changed the truth of God into a lie, and *worshipped* and served [honored] the *creature* [man] more than the *Creator* [God], who is blessed forever. Amen" (Romans 1:25, emphasis mine).

This folly was due to the same error that millions are making right now. They turned to the realm of familiar spirits for guidance, just as people are doing today.

There is one account in particular that brings out what I want to convey. It is found in Acts 16:16-19:

> And it came to pass, as we went to prayer, a certain damsel possessed with a *spirit of divination* [familiar spirit] met us, which brought her masters much gain by soothsaying [psychic predictions]: The same followed Paul and us, and cried, saying, "These men are the servants of the most high God, Which shew unto us the way of salvation." And this did she many days. But Paul, being grieved, turned and said to the spirit, "I command thee in the name of Jesus Christ to come out of her." And he came out the same hour. And when her masters saw that the hope of their gains was gone, they caught Paul and Silas, and drew them into the marketplace and unto the rulers. (emphasis mine)

These verses show four things that are *critical* to understanding the nature and aim of the New Age movement:

> 1. The spirit was the *source* of her power, *not* some latent faculty inherent in the human makeup. When it went, her ability was *gone*.

> 2. The spirit was accurate to a high degree. Otherwise she would not have brought her masters "much gain." You don't become a success with a poor showing.

> 3. Paul and the spirit were *not on the same side*. This is quite evident by the fact that he cast it out of her.

> 4. Most important of all, the spirit tried to *identify itself with God*. When it followed Paul and Silas, it was saying the truth, "These men show us the way of salvation." By doing this, the spirit could continue its practice of deceiving all concerned and perhaps later undo what Paul's ministry had accomplished.

These spirits are doing the same thing today. This girl, no doubt, believed that it was her *inner divinity* giving her the information that was so effective in *aiding* the community. The truth of the matter is, when you say you have connected with your inner divinity and that you are God, sadly, you have joined the ranks of those who, "Professing themselves to be wise [knowing the truth], they became fools [absurd], and changed the glory of the *uncorruptible* God into an image made like to *corruptible* man" (Romans 1:22-23, emphasis mine).

Swami Muktananda was one of the most admired and respected New Age leaders during the 1970s and early 1980s. He was thought by many to be the virtual embodiment of the *God-realized* master. He told His disciples:

> Kneel to your own self. Honor and worship your

own Being. Chant the mantra always going on within you. Meditate on your own self. God dwells within you as you.[12]

When Muktananda died in 1982, one of his closest followers revealed that his master "ended as a feeble-minded, sadistic tyrant luring devout little girls to his bed every night with promises of grace and self-realization."[13] Without realizing he was echoing the truth of the verses just quoted, he concluded:

> There is no absolute assurance that enlightenment necessitates the moral virtue of a person. There is no guarantee against the weakness of anger, lust, and greed in the human soul. The enlightened are on an equal footing with the ignorant in the struggle against their own evil.[14]

It is very clear that the metaphysical explosion that our society is currently immersed in is a continuation of what Leviticus 19:31 warned against:

> Regard not them that have familiar spirits, neither seek after wizards [metaphysicians], to be *defiled* by them: I am the Lord your God. (emphasis mine)

On this basis alone, Christians have a duty to challenge the validity of the New Age message that *we are God*.

ELEVEN

THE END OF THE AGE?

THE subject covered in this chapter has traditionally been called the *Apocalypse* or the revelation of the writings that disclose the end times. In the Bible, this end time period is referred to as "the day of the Lord."* Bible scholars refer to it as the time of *the Great Tribulation*. Some Christians believe that the events foretold throughout the Bible actually have already happened in the first century AD. Such a view is known as preterism. But I believe there are certain aspects of these prophecies that have not occurred yet and are even occurring now. I would ask those that hold the preterist view to be willing to examine the evidence I present in this chapter.

During this time (the end of the age), the one Christians refer to as the *Antichrist* will make his appearance. The apostle Paul refers to this personality as "the son of perdition" and the

---

* Several verses in the Bible refer to "the day of the Lord": Acts 2:20, I Corinthians 5:5, II Corinthians 1:14, I Thessalonians 5:2 and II Peter 3:10. There are also many in the Old Testament.

"man of sin" (II Thessalonians 2:3). The term antichrist actually stands for *ante*-christ meaning more of a substitute than an opposite. In other words, Satan wants to masquerade as the Christ himself and take his seat in the temple—the ultimate blasphemy where he says, *I Am God.*

When the time is right, Satan will come in person in a man who is completely yielded to him. This man (the Antichrist) will unite the world under a *counterfeit* spiritual system that blasphemes God and His plan. We read in Revelation 13:5-6:

> And there was given unto him a mouth speaking great things and blasphemies; and power was given unto him to continue forty and two months. And he opened his mouth in blasphemy against God, to blaspheme His name, and His tabernacle, and them that dwell in heaven.

Ultimately, this impostor will be knocked from power by the *literal* Second Coming of Jesus Christ at the end of the seven-year tribulation period. In II Thessalonians 2:8-10, we read:

> And then shall that Wicked be revealed, whom the Lord shall consume with the spirit of His mouth, and shall destroy with the *brightness of His coming:* Even him, whose coming is after the working of Satan with all power and signs and lying wonders, And with all deceivableness of unrighteousness in them that perish; because they received not the love of the truth, that they might be saved. (emphasis mine)

After the destruction of this deceiver and his false program, the true Savior (Jesus Christ) will set up His kingdom on earth and rule in what is referred to as the Millennium, a time of *true* rest and peace on the earth.

The Times and Seasons

In light of these prophetic warnings, the advent of the New Age movement takes on a very special significance. The apostle Paul spoke of the day of the Lord in reference to "the times and seasons" in I Thessalonians 5:1-2.

He was making reference to the Old Testament book of Daniel. King Nebuchadnezzar had a dream concerning the Gentile kingdoms which would begin with his kingdom, Babylon, and continue through Media-Persia, Greece, Rome and ten future kingdoms. Before Daniel interpreted the dream, he made it known that God is responsible for the changes in dispensations, which he calls "the times and seasons":

> Daniel answered and said, "Blessed be the name of God for ever and ever: for wisdom and might are His: And *He changeth the times and the seasons:* He removeth kings, and setteth up kings: He giveth wisdom unto the wise, and knowledge to them that know understanding: He revealeth the deep and secret things: He knoweth what is in the darkness, and the light dwelleth with Him. (Daniel 2:20-22, emphasis added)

When asked by the Apostles in Acts 1:6 whether God would restore the kingdom at that time (bringing in the millennium), Jesus replied in verse 7, "it is not for you to know the times or the seasons." It is very apparent that this phrase is connected to changes in dispensations. In light of this, study the verses in I Thessalonians 5:1-6 very carefully where the apostle Paul states:

> But of the *times and the seasons,* brethren, ye have no need that I write unto you. For yourselves know perfectly that the day of the Lord so cometh as a thief in the night. For when they shall say, Peace and safety; then sudden destruction cometh upon

them, as travail upon a woman with child; and they
shall not escape. *But ye, brethren, are not in darkness,
that that day should overtake you as a thief.* Ye are all
the children of light, and the children of the day:
we are not of the night, nor of darkness. Therefore
let us not sleep, as do others; but let us watch and
be sober. (emphasis mine)

Paul is saying that the end of the age will come upon the
world like a thief in the night—it will sneak up on people. Then he
contrasts two groups. "But ye brethren, are not in darkness [igno-
rance] that that day should overtake you as a thief [unaware]" (vs.
4). He is saying that believers in Christ will have the information
available to them to prepare for "that day."

Paul goes on to say, "Ye are all the children of light, and the
children of the day" (vs. 5). Those who walk in the light can see
both where they are going and what is coming ahead. He warns
against spiritual slumber and drunkenness which could lead
to a person being overtaken by that day unaware. "Therefore
let us not sleep, as do others; but let us watch and be sober"
(vs. 6). The word *sober* here means "alert" or "aware." If one is
instructed to watch and be aware there must be something to
watch for—otherwise, Paul's admonition would be useless. The
reason Paul said, "Ye have no need that I write unto you," is
because the forewarning of when that day would arrive came
from Jesus Christ Himself.

For *Many* Shall Come in My Name

My research has brought me to a point where the full implication
of Paul's words are surprisingly real. I believe the Bible contains
an important signal that the changes of times and seasons may
indeed be at hand. In Matthew 24:3-5, which is a chapter dealing
with the tribulation period, Jesus spoke these revealing words to
His disciples concerning the signs of His coming and the end
of the world (age):

> And as He sat upon the mount of Olives, the disciples
> came unto Him privately, saying, Tell us, *when shall
> these things be?* and what shall be *the sign* [indication] of
> thy coming, and of the *end of the world* [age]? And Jesus
> answered and said unto them, Take heed that no man
> deceive you. *For many shall come in My name, saying, I
> am Christ; and shall deceive many.*" (emphasis mine)

In the past, I have heard two basic ways of interpreting verse
5—"for many shall come in my name, saying, 'I am Christ;' and
shall deceive many." The first interpretation is that there will
be various ones claiming to be the returned Jesus Christ. The
other view, which has gained greater acceptance in the last
ten or fifteen years, is that a number of messiah figures would
appear and gather followers to themselves in a fashion similar
to Jim Jones or Bhagwan Shree Rajneesh. I now feel both of
these interpretations may be incorrect. It is in light of some
predominant New Age viewpoints that these verses take on
major significance.

A basic tenet of New Age thinking is that of *the Master Jesus.*
Adherents to this idea believe that during the unrecorded period
of His life, Jesus traveled to various occult centers and Mystery
Schools in such places as Tibet, India, Persia, and Egypt where
He learned the metaphysical secrets of the ages. Thus, they claim
He spent seventeen years of travel on a pilgrimage of higher consciousness. According to this theory Jesus of Nazareth became
the Master Jesus, one who has gained mastery over the physical
world by becoming one with his higher self.

You will recall that one of the terms that New Agers regularly
use for the higher self is the *Christ consciousness.* To them, Christ
is not a person, but a state-of-being. Excerpts from the following
New Age sources explain it this way:

> Jesus Christ educated His followers to discern the
> real man. He taught that there is a power in man
> that gives him authority over the things of the

world. This principle is the higher self, the spiritual man, the Christ.[1]

The Christ Consciousness or Christ Principle represents the idea of a Saviour, but not, as taught in orthodox religions, a physical, material person. Jesus became the Saviour as He rose to the heights of His inner powers and became a True Son of God. . . . In other words, when Jesus, the man, was ready, the Christ Principle or Consciousness took over and predominated.[2]

After reading innumerable such statements in New Age material, I decided to take a closer look at Matthew 24:5. What I found astounded me. The Greek word for *many* in this verse is *polus* which means a *very great* or *sore* number, as in millions and millions. A term derived from this word is *hoi polloi*, which translates *the masses*. The Greek words *for shall come in my name* means they shall come claiming to represent what He represents by using His name or authority. Therefore, Matthew 24:5 is saying that a *very great* number of people shall come claiming to represent what He represents, but are in fact, deceiving people. In light of *come in my name*, consider the following remarks taken from a variety of New Age sources:

Jesus was an historical person, a human being; Christ, the Christos. is an eternal transpersonal condition of being. Jesus did not say that this higher state of consciousness realized in him was his alone for all time. Nor did he call us to worship him. Rather, he called us to follow him, to follow in his steps, to learn from him, from his example.[3]

Jesus was one soul who reached the state of Christ consciousness, there have been many others. He symbolized the blueprint we must follow. . . . The way is open to everyone to become a Christ

> by achieving the Christ Consciousness through walking the same path He walked. . . . He simply and beautifully demonstrated the pattern.[4]

> The significance of incarnation and resurrection is not that Jesus was a human like us but rather that *we are gods like him—or* at least have the potential to be. The significance of Jesus is not as a vehicle of salvation but as a model of perfection.[5]

> Jesus was aware of himself as a finished specimen of the new humanity which is to come—the new humanity which is to inherit the earth, establish the Kingdom, usher in the New Age.[6]

This view, then, is that Jesus is a *model* of what the New Age or Aquarian person is to become. I would say these statements can be called *coming in His name* or claiming to represent what He represents.

Now let us look at the second part of verse 5 in Matthew 24, "saying I am Christ." Again, we find a multitude of statements such as the following:

> Every man is an individual Christ; this is the teaching for the New Age. The experiences of contacting the Christ Self and the subsequent vibrational lifting *are not to be reserved for a favored few.* Every person in the world, sooner or later, will receive this lifting action. *No one* will be left out or left behind. *Everyone* will receive the benefit of this step in *human evolution.*" (emphasis mine)[7]

> Could it be that many Christians have been looking for "the Christ" in all the wrong places? Could it be that when Jesus said "no man knoweth the hour" of his return, it was because the return of the Christ comes *now*, within us, and is beyond

space and time? Jesus may have been hinting at this when he told us the kingdom of God is within you—not in some time, nor in some place, but *within*. When we look within, through meditation and the expansion of consciousness, we move beyond time, and meet face-to-face with the Christ.[8]

The Christ is You. You are the one who is to come—each of you. Each and every one of you![9]

Christhood is not something to come at a point in the future when you are more evolved. Christhood is—right now! I am the Christ of God. You are the Christ of God.[10]

Even more specific evidence ties the New Age into Jesus' prophecy. In Luke 21:7-8, we find the same discourse as in Matthew 24:3-5. Again, note the warning:

And they asked him, saying, Master, but when shall these things be? and what sign will there be when these things shall come to pass? And he said, Take heed that ye be not deceived: for many shall come in My name, saying, I am *Christ*; and the time draweth near; go ye not therefore after them. (Luke 21:7-8)

Notice "Christ" is italicized in verse 8, meaning that it was not in the original manuscript. The translators of the King James Bible probably thought it awkward that it said, "Many shall come saying, I am." Probably for the sake of clarity and to be consistent with Matthew 24, the translators added the word "Christ." It is very interesting that New Agers refer to themselves (or their higher selves) as the "I AM," (one of the names of God). Note the following:

The first experience of unification with the Christ consciousness may come with the initial crossing

of the psychic barrier and contact with the Christ
Self or I AM Self.[11]

This Inner Self is called by many names such as:
God-self, Higher-self, Christ Consciousness, I-AM,
Buddah Nature, and many others.[12]

This I AM is God . . . this I AM is You. . . . Universe
and Individual Consciousness. . . . God knowing
Itself as God, God knowing Itself as You, and You
knowing Yourself as God.[13]

So what Jesus may have been saying is many shall be saying
"I AM."

Because of these statements, I firmly believe what Jesus
Christ was prophesying in Matthew and Luke was the current
New Age movement when it reaches its full fruition world-wide.
He clearly stated that just before His physical return a huge
number of people will proclaim their own personal divinity and
that "many" (polus) will deceive—not some, but "many." There
was a good reason for Him to preface these prophesies with the
warning, "Take heed that no man deceive you." These people
will be offering a spiritual message that will look, feel, and sound
like it is of Jesus Christ but is not.

The Man of Sin

Paul declared that during this time "the man of sin, the son
of perdition" would proclaim himself to be "God" (II Thessalonians 2:3-4). One channeled source made it clear that the
term *Christ* will mean both the "Christ energy" and a man
that will *personify* that energy. Consider the following New
Age statements:

The reappearance of the Avatar [world teacher],
by whatever name he may be known, has been

prophesied in many religions as well as in the esoteric [occultic] tradition. A major manifestation is expected in connection with the Aquarian age.[14]

[A] Saviour appears every two thousand years (more or less) for the different ages. Each Saviour brings the tone or keynote for the age.[15]

Literally, the Second Coming of the Christ is the discovery within each one of you, and all of mankind, of his or her divinity, his or her Christ-hood.... The only thing which will call for "an individual" representing the Christ appearing on your planet, will be for those doubting Thomases, those who refuse to acknowledge their divinity, who have it invested solely in one man. *They will need one man to appear who they will listen to,* who will then turn their attention back on themselves and get about the business of waking up! (emphasis mine)[16]

I believe that this coming Aquarian Messiah could possibly be the son of perdition that II Thessalonians speaks of and that the New Age movement would be his *spiritual platform*–too many things fit together to ignore this possible scenario. Daniel 8:23 states that this man will be a master of "dark" sayings. In Hebrew, this translates as one skilled in cunning and ambiguous speech. Keep this in mind as you read the following quote:

The coming one will not be Christian, a Hindu, a Buddhist, not an American, Jew, Italian or Russian—his title is not important, he is for all humanity, to unite all religions, philosophies and nations.[17]

The only one who could accomplish this interspiritual unity on a global scale would be the one who fits the description of the person mentioned in Daniel. That is why all this effort to saturate society with meditation is going on right now. When this man comes forward, all those in touch with their Higher Selves (familiar spirits) are going to automatically recognize him as "the Coming One" and give him their allegiance. He will have a ready made constituency, many in key positions, to help him reconstruct society. This will be the final culmination of the paradigm shift.

The potential *power* of this deception is keenly brought out in the following observation made by a disciple of Indian Guru Rajneesh and also reflects what the Antichrist will do with humanity:

> Something had happened to Rajneesh that made him unlike other men. He had undergone some change—enlightenment, the rising of kundalini—and his being had been altered in palpable [noticeable] ways. The change in him in turn affected his sannyasins [disciples] and created a *persistent and catalyzing resonance between them.* (emphasis mine)[18]

The Bible predicts that the Antichrist shall perform "lying wonders." Alice Bailey described "the Work" of this New Age Christ very explicitly:

> The work of the Christ (two thousand years ago) was to proclaim certain great possibilities and the existence of great powers. His work when He reappears will be to prove the fact of these possibilities and to reveal the true nature and potency of man.[19]

A perfect example of this in practice is found in a book by New Age healer and author Ron Roth. He told of being at a conference years ago, which featured the famous healer Agnes Sanford as the featured speaker. There were three thousand people in attendance altogether. Roth explained that a bad drought had hit the Southern California area where the conference was being held, and many people were concerned about its effects.

When Sanford took the stage, she addressed this dilemma:

> I'm sick and tired of hearing this. Everyone of you
> tells me you are on the spiritual path, and you
> complain about the fact that it isn't raining. All
> right, now take a lesson.. . .I declare that the rains
> are now coming from Southern Mexico.[20]

Only a few hours later, according to Roth, it started to rain
and wouldn't quit for the entire weekend. Some people asked
her to make it stop, and this was her reply:

> "No," she said. "I gave you awareness of your power.
> You stop it."[21]

What did Sanford mean by "your power"? The answer is
found in her book, *The Healing Light*. In it, she gives her view
of "the spiritual path" she referred to in the talk. She explains:

> Only the amount of God that we can get in us will
> work for us.[22]

> Learning to live in the kingdom of Heaven is
> learning to turn on the light of God within.[23]

> It is for us to learn His will, to seek the simplicity
> and the beauty of the laws that set free His power.[24]

How *does* one set God's power free? Through meditation!
Sanford explains:

> I have learned to combine the sacramental with the
> meditative approach. . . . And in the same way we
> bid our conscious minds be still.[25]

As with the other figures you have been reading about in
this book, she opened up a channel to a supernatural source:

> We may be conscious of an inrushing current of
> energy, like electricity. . . . a spiritual light-vibration
> penetrates and fills every cell of the body. In other
> words, we are porous like a sponge and filled with
> God.[26]

She summed up her entire philosophy, which she was conveying at that conference that Roth attended, in the following
manner:

> Thus we are "part God.". . . Knowing then that we
> are part of God, that His life within us is an active
> energy and that He works through the laws of our
> bodies, let us study to adjust and conform ourselves
> to those laws.[27]

In her autobiography, *Sealed Orders*, Sanford credits her spiritual
affinities to a lecture she attended and books written by the famed
New Thought exponent, Emmett Fox, whom she said had an "enlightened understanding" which "thrilled" her soul.[28]

Fox believed, as all *good* New Agers do, that God was "Infinite
Mind" and "Substance Itself" and worked through "spiritual
influx" and "Cosmic Law" made available through "scientific
prayer" [meditation].[29] Now spiritual influx is the idea that these
energies and powers come through mystical states of awareness
and enable you to manifest (like shamanism) your desires.

What Roth was recounting at that conference was a small scale
version of what the man of sin will do on a world-wide scale. This
is what Alice Bailey meant by "reveal the true nature and potency
of man!" However, it's not *really* man doing this—it's what the
Bible refers to as "lying wonders." The man of sin will do this
on an enormous scale. He will seem to work great miracles to
show everyone that they are all "christs" and that they all have
this great "power," or as Bailey said, "potency" within them.

In light of this, consider the following story of a woman's
encounter with a "healer":

Instantly my body felt as though it were filled with
white light and I became weak in my knees and I
started swaying. Soon, I became unable to stand, and
someone helped me to sit in a chair. Thereafter, I felt
extreme heat beating down into my head, particularly
on the left side. All during this experience, I was
completely conscious and my body was filled with
waves of ecstasy. It was an oceanic feeling, much
greater than orgasm, since it involved my whole
being. I remember breathing deeply to support
the increased energy in my system. I was so happy
that I began to moan in pleasure and then to laugh
aloud. I had heard about and visualized white light
before, but had never experienced being totally
infused with it. I immediately made an association
to the healing power of Jesus Christ, and had *no
doubts* that this was the nature of the energy being
transmitted to me.[30]

The man that did this to her was a *New Ager*. This shows
that even known occultists have the power—through familiar
spirits—to mimic what most people would consider to be of God.

Bailey also revealed: "The ground is being prepared at this
time for the great restoration which the Christ will engineer."[31]
In the context of that statement, she informs us that what will
be restored are the "ancient Mysteries."[32] These are the same as
the Mystery Schools.

The origin of the Antichrist's religious system is revealed by
the apostle John in Revelation 17:5:

And upon her forehead was a name written,
MYSTERY, BABYLON THE GREAT, THE MOTHER OF
HARLOTS AND ABOMINATIONS OF THE EARTH.

Another word for Babylon in the Old Testament was
Chaldea. The Chaldeans were renowned for their use of the

metaphysical arts. They were the first Mystery School. Daniel 4:7 says, "Then came in the magicians, the astrologers, *the Chaldeans* and the soothsayers." The Old Testament book of Leviticus makes reference to those who listen to familiar spirits as "whoring after them," and Deuteronomy 18 refers to the practices of metaphysics as "abominations" in God's sight. This *Mystery Babylon*, then, would be the *original source* or "mother" of what is now New Age metaphysics.

Thus, when John identifies the Antichrist's spiritual format, he is making reference to the city and people that first spawned occultism in ancient times. *All* of the other Mystery Schools came out of Babylon, teaching basically the *same thing–the Ancient Wisdom*. John saw it as one unbroken line throughout history culminating in the Antichrist's rule when hundreds of millions are given over to familiar spirits.

It is the correlation between what the Bible says about the Antichrist and his design and what the New Age says about its own intentions that leads me to believe we could be observing the unfolding of Bible prophecy.

The Blood of the Saints

One of the main tenets of New Age thought is peace, goodwill, and the unity of all humanity. Remember, the Age of Aquarius is to be the *Age of Oneness*. In context with this idea, the New Age term *cleansing* is quite disturbing. A number of books make reference to those who are *laggards* when the New Age reaches its maturity. New Age leaders consider these resisters as eventually the only hindrance in allowing this global oneness to occur:

> Remnants of the Fifth Root Race [untransformed humanity] will continue to survive in the initial stages of the new Cosmic Cycle, but unless they increase their awareness or consciousness to the Higher Mind and the tempo of spirituality, they will be removed from the Life Stream of the Race.[33]

Unity-motivated souls will respond to His [the New Age Messiah's] call, their inner drive for spiritual world unity will synchronize with higher energy. People opposing the recognition of the Christ may struggle intensely, but it will not be prolonged. The Christ energy by then will be so strong people will be *dealt with* according to their own individualized karma and *their ability and desire to assimilate this accelerated energy.* (emphasis mine)[34] The final appearance of the Christ will be an evolutionary event. It will be the disappearance of egocentric [lower self], subhuman man and the ascension of God-centered Man. A new race, a new species, will inhabit the Earth—people who collectively have the stature of consciousness that Jesus had.[35]

Even Alice Bailey herself, who personified New Age consciousness, backs what these previous quotes imply:

The new era is coming; the new ideals, the new civilization, the new modes of life, of education, of religious presentation and of government are slowly precipitating and naught can stop them. They can, however, be delayed by the *reactionary types of people*, by the ultra-conservative and closed minds. . . . *They are the ones* who can and do hold back the hour of liberation. A spiritual fluidity, a willingness to let all preconceived ideas and ideals go, as well as all beloved tendencies, cultivated habits of thought and every determined effort to make the world conform to a pattern which seems to the individual the best because, to him, the most enticing—these must all be brought under the power of death. (emphasis mine)[36]

If one understands the rationale behind these statements, then it becomes clear what they are talking about. Those who will accept the *Christ consciousness* can stay—those who *won't—must go*. The quote about people's "ability and desire" to assimilate the "Christ energy" as the determining factor in their fate is very thought provoking.

Barbara Marx Hubbard, a major New Age proponent and a supporter of Marianne Williamson's Department of Peace efforts in Washington, DC says there must be a "selection process" for those "who refuse to see themselves and others as a part of God [Hubbard's New Age God]." She states:

> He [God] describes, therefore, the necessity of a "selection process" that will select out resistant individuals who "choose" not to evolve.[37]

> Human must become Divine. That is the law.[38]

You will recall David Spangler's words from Chapter 10, about Lucifer being the angel of man's "inner evolution." Christians know Lucifer to be Satan, the Adversary, and II Thessalonians 2:9 informs us that Satan is the one who will empower the Antichrist. Those defying the Antichrist will really be defying Satan—and they will suffer dearly for it.

Persecution and death is *predicted* in the Bible for those who won't fall into line during the Antichrist's rule. The parallel between what the Bible says about this period and the statements above are striking. The following prophecies reveal what is in store for those who will preach the *real* Jesus Christ and the Gospel of the *true* kingdom during this time. Jesus said in Matthew 24:9:

> Then shall they deliver you up to be afflicted, and *shall kill you:* and ye shall be hated of all nations for my name's sake. (emphasis mine)

"They" are the many who are coming in His name claiming to be "christs." Revelation says of this period:

> And when He had opened the fifth seal, I saw under the altar the souls of them that were *slain for the word of God,* and for the testimony which they held: And they cried with a loud voice, saying, "How long, O Lord, holy and *true,* dost thou not judge and avenge *our blood* on them that dwell on the earth?" (Revelation 6:9-10, emphasis mine)

> And I saw thrones, and they sat upon them, and judgment was given unto them: and I saw the souls of them *that were beheaded for the witness of Jesus, and for the word of God,* and which had not worshipped the beast, neither *his image,* neither had received his mark upon their foreheads, or in their hands; and they lived and reigned with Christ a thousand years. (Revelation 20:4, emphasis mine)

The following verse lends credence that this will be on an individual spiritual basis:

> And ye shall be betrayed both by parents, and brethren, and kinfolks, and friends; and some of you shall they cause to be put to death. (Luke 21:16)

This implies that a family member or a friend may be turned over to be dealt with *for their own good.* It will be seen as an altruistic act.

This view would most likely infuriate anyone involved with or attracted to New Age spirituality. After all, nowhere do you find New Agers saying they are going to kill anybody. It is left rather vague about how anyone will be removed. But the following channeled words by Neale Donald Walsch's "God" explain the rationale for what most people would consider outrageous and impossible. Listen to his "God":

> So the first thing you have to understand—as I've already explained to you—is that Hitler didn't *hurt* anyone. In a sense, he didn't *inflict* suffering, he ended it.[39]

> There is no "death." Life goes on forever and ever. Life is. You simply change form. . . . After you change form, consequences cease to exist. There is just Knowing.[40]

> The real issue is whether Hitler's actions where [were] "wrong." Yet I have said over and over again that there is no "right" or "wrong" in the universe. Now your thought that Hitler was a monster is based on the fact that he ordered the killing of millions of people, correct? What if I told you that what you call "death" is the *greatest thing that could happen to anyone*—what then?. . . Shall we therefore punish Bre'r Fox for throwing Bre'r Rabbit into the briar patch? (emphasis mine)[41]

This is a very revealing statement. Traditional morality has been virtually turned on its head here. In other words, according to the *higher consciousness* that Walsch is in tune with, killing people could actually be doing them a favor! But would Walsch think this is profound higher wisdom if he himself was shivering sick and starving in a cattle car bound for Auschwitz. Would he have a smile on his face if he were stripped naked and herded into a gas chamber to face a gruesome, agonizing death? I think not!

But incredibly, Walsch is one of the featured speakers in *The Secret* (see page 103) which is now sweeping the Western world in popularity. In *The Secret*, Walsch is described as a "modern-day spiritual messenger"[42] and his *Conversations with God* books (including the one from which the previous quotes about Hitler were taken) are called "groundbreaking."

Could there have been the same spiritual component to Hitler's persecution of humanity in Europe? Most likely.

Consider the following evidence. The swastika, the main symbol of Nazism, is an age-old Hindu symbol that is still found on many temples throughout India. The word is not even German, but Sanskrit—Svastika—meaning "that which is excellent."[43] A New Age book has described its meaning as representing "the final stage in which the chakra is active, developed, opened, and energized by awakened kundalini energy."[44] Thus, the very banner of Nazism stood for the energy that underlies the whole New Age movement. New Agers even acknowledge this. David Spangler makes reference in one of his books to "...the Nazi movement, which had many roots in occultism."[45] The swastika symbol was also prominently displayed on Madame Blavatsky's personal brooch, in exactly the same style as the Nazi one (tilting at an angle to the right) decades before the Nazi Party was even formed. One can also see the parallel between Nazism and the Ancient Wisdom in the Hindu caste system, with its Brahmin (aryan) caste and its lower *untouchable* caste. The Nazis also took the term Aryan—literally, *the worthy race*—from Hinduism.[46] The word has nothing to do with ancient Germany as many believe, but is a Hindu word meaning noble or superior.

Is the Church Spiritual Israel?

Matthew 24:14 states that "the gospel of the kingdom shall be preached in all the world" during those seven years. What is this message that the Antichrist will try to stamp out with all his might, and who are those who will preach that message that Jesus Christ is coming to set up His kingdom?

In Luke 21:8, the Lord tells His disciples that when "many" come claiming to represent His character saying, "I am Christ," or "I am God," then the time of His coming will be close. When "the time" does come, the Lord will come back with "power and great glory" (vs. 27) and "as a snare" (vs. 35). Jesus Christ's kingdom comes upon "the whole earth" (vs. 35). The man of sin (Antichrist) is then unseated and destroyed by "the brightness of His [Christ's] coming" (II Thessalonians 2:8). Then the kingdom will be established in Israel as promised. See Ezekiel 36:22-38 and 43:1-9.

One fact concerning Bible prophecy is quite clear. When Jesus Christ returns to set up the kingdom of heaven, it is the *Antichrist* who has had dominion over the earth the previous seven years—*not* the Body of Christ.

This did not happen in the first century AD. Nero Caesar did not have dominion over the world. There were other great empires at the time in Persia, India, and China that Nero had no influence over.

Some people in various Christian camps believe that the church is in fact *spiritual Israel* and the promises made to national or ethnic Israel will never again apply to her, but only to the body of Christ. In other words, God is finished forever with Israel. But according to Revelation 7:2-4, this cannot be the case. It says:

> And I saw another angel ascending from the east, having the seal of the living God: and he cried with a loud voice to the four angels, to whom it was given to hurt the earth and the sea, Saying, "Hurt not the earth, neither the sea, nor the trees, till we have sealed the servants of our God in their foreheads." And I heard the number of them which were sealed: and there were sealed an hundred and forty and four thousand of *all the tribes of the children of Israel*. (emphasis mine)

This also did not happen in the first century AD. It is not speaking metaphorically because the tribes are then named. If the church is now spiritual Israel, what spiritual tribe does a Christian belong to? The answer is *none* because these verses are talking about 144,000 ethnic Jews who will preach the true Gospel of the real kingdom in the days before Christ's return. In Luke 1:31-33 the angel Gabriel told Mary:

> And, behold, thou shall conceive in thy womb, and
> bring forth a son, and shalt call His name Jesus. He
> shall be great, and shall be called the Son of the
> Highest: and the Lord God shall give unto Him
> *the throne of His father David:* And *He shall reign over*
> *the house of Jacob for ever;* and of His kingdom there
> shall be no end. (emphasis mine)

The "throne of His father David" and the "house of Jacob"
both refer to the nation of Israel, not the church. In Isaiah 2:3,
it says "out of Zion [the nation of Israel] shall go forth the law
and the word of the Lord from Jerusalem."

I believe the literal approach is the best way to understand
this controversy. Israel is a nation once again. She is an entity,
not a scattered people. The things that are prophesied concerning the Jewish people throughout the New Testament are just
in the right position now for these to be fulfilled.

Bailey's Goal Realized

Alice Bailey once made the following prediction:

> The education and reorientation of the advanced
> human being must find its place in our mass
> education . . . The experienced voice of the eastern
> wisdom comes to us with one word:—Meditation.
> The question naturally arises: "Is that all?" and the
> answer is: "Yes."[47]

Well, this is exactly what has happened. As I have shown
throughout my book, virtually every major endeavor of human
activity has been seeded with meditation methods and practices
that are in tune with Aquarian spirituality. This is a fact that
anyone can independently verify. Such flowering of mysticism
is unprecedented. Never has such a variety of mystical options
been simultaneously available to the general populace.

Incredibly, as New Age influence has grown stronger, the Christian response has grown weaker to the point of virtually drying up. If you look at the *apologetics* section in many Christian bookstores, you will find numerous titles on atheism, evolution, Mormonism, some on Islam, but little or none specifically on the New Age. Christians need to be aware for the sake of their families that this is something that poses the potential to greatly impact anyone in their circle of friends or loved ones. In one Reiki magazine, I found an advertisement for a Reiki teddy bear, which said: "This teddy bear can be infused with Reiki energy and given to a child."[48] This is a stunning illustration that New Age influence should not be dismissed as mere silliness. It is anything but silly!

TWELVE

SALVATION AND THE NEW AGE

And with all deceivableness of unrighteousness
in them that perish; because they received not
the love of the truth, that they might be saved.
(II Thessalonians 2:10)

Who Will Be Among "Them That Perish?"

If you have always wondered what church to join or whether
you have been *good enough* to get into heaven, then understand
that the only thing that really *counts* is whether or not you are a
member of the Body of Christ. The way of entering the Body of
Christ is by believing the "gospel of your salvation."

Perhaps you may be asking, why do I need salvation? And
that leads us to something that is very unpopular these days—
the idea that you (and every human being) are an unrighteous
person. If at first you find this idea offensive and unacceptable,
then consider the qualifications for being unrighteous.

> Being filled with all unrighteousness, fornication,
> wickedness, covetousness, maliciousness; full of
> envy, murder, debate, deceit, malignity; whisperers,
> backbiters, haters of God, despiteful, proud, boasters,
> inventors of evil things, disobedient to parents, without

understanding, covenant breakers, without natural affection, implacable, unmerciful: Who knowing the judgment of God, that they which commit such things are worthy of death, not only do the same, but have pleasure in them that do them (Romans 1:29-32).

This means if you have ever in your life:

→ been greedy
→ made trouble for someone
→ been jealous of anybody for *any* reason
→ gotten mad at or argued with someone because they did not agree with you
→ lied to cover up your wrongdoing or to get something
→ played a dirty trick on someone
→ gossiped or said bad things about others
→ broken a promise or a deal
→ bragged about yourself
→ looked down on anyone
→ been stubborn on settling an issue
→ lacked compassion towards someone
→ done other activities of this kind, or even been *sympathetic* with someone else doing them, then you are *unrighteous*. These things do not apply in just extreme cases but common, everyday instances too.

Can We Be Righteous Before God?

Jesus Christ gave the requirements to be counted righteous before God in and of yourself in Matthew 22:37-40:

Jesus said unto him, "Thou shalt love the Lord thy God with all thy heart, and with all thy soul, and with all thy mind. This is the first and great commandment. And the second is like unto it. Thou shalt love thy neighbor as thyself. On these two commandments hang all the law and the prophets."

That means you would love God and everybody around you *exactly* as you love yourself. This would also be something you *successfully did your entire life,* not just *tried* to do. Hardest of all, you would have to do this not only in *deed* but also in *thought* because "Man looketh on the outward appearance, but the Lord looketh on the heart" (I Samuel 16:7).

If we loved everyone as we love ourselves, we would not be *capable* of the sins mentioned earlier. People love *themselves* first and foremost. Not only is this evident in our daily lives and the lives of those around us, but it is also a pronouncement of the Bible, "For all have sinned, and come short of the glory of God" (Romans 3:23). Again in Romans 3:10, "As it is written, There is none righteous [innocent], no, not one."

Good Works or Grace

The New Age and Christianity definitely disagree on the answer to this dilemma of human imperfection. Metaphysics puts forth the doctrine of reincarnation and karma where the soul, through good works, evolves through many lives to a point where it can free itself from earthly bondage and become self-realized, united with the universe which is seen as God, but in reality is the realm of familiar spirits.

On the other hand, Christ's Gospel offers salvation to mankind through *grace* (unmerited favor). Romans 3:24 says, "Being justified freely by His grace through the redemption that is in Christ Jesus." Then in Romans 6:23 we read, "For the wages of sin is death; but the gift of God is eternal life through Jesus Christ our Lord."

This "gift" is not earned or given as a reward for earnest effort or good intentions. Ephesians 2:8-9 states clearly:

> For by grace are ye saved through faith; and that not of yourselves: it is the gift of God: Not of works, lest any man should boast.

The reason human effort does not work is because man is "dead in trespasses and sins" (Ephesians 2:1). The word *works* is translated "actions" or "doings." This can either mean good deeds or engaging in religious rituals.

In metaphysics, the very word *karma* translates to mean *actions* or *works*. By your own effort and doings you are supposed to advance spiritually. If you are "dead" spiritually, as the Bible states, the concept of karma would be like trying to start a car without a battery.

New Age's Clash with Christianity

Where Christianity and the New Age clash most decidedly is in the nature of the person and work of Jesus Christ. The New Age sees Him as a great master, a way-shower to Christ consciousness, a metaphysical guru—someone who is the prototype of the Aquarian Age man.

The way the Bible describes Him can be summed up in the following two verses:

> But these are written, that ye might believe that Jesus is the Christ, the Son of God; and that believing ye might have life through His name. (John 20:31)

> But we see Jesus, who was made a little lower than the angels, for the suffering of death, crowned with glory and honour; that He by the grace of God should taste death for every man. (Hebrews 2:9)

This verse in Hebrews reveals to us that Christ's sacrifice was a substitution for all mankind. In other words, He paid with His own blood the price (which is death and separation from God) for our sin. He died to take the penalty we deserved:

> In whom we have *redemption through His blood,* the forgiveness of sins, according to the riches of His grace. (Ephesians 1:7, emphasis mine)

Romans 5:9-10 goes on to explain:

> Much more then, being now *justified* by *His blood,*
> we shall be saved from wrath through Him. For if,
> when we were enemies, we were reconciled to God
> by the *death of His Son,* much more, being reconciled,
> we shall be saved by His life. (emphasis mine)

As we read earlier in Ephesians 2:8, "For by grace are ye saved through *faith.*" It is faith in the sacrifice of Jesus Christ.

The Bad News and the Good News

W ell, the bad news is that there is *nothing* you can do about your sinfulness. But the good news is that God tells you that His grace is sufficient to save you. Grace is God doing for man what man is unable to do for himself—not man doing for God. Romans 4:4-5 explains:

> Now to him that worketh is the reward not reckoned
> of grace, but of debt. But to him that worketh not,
> but believeth on Him that justifieth the ungodly,
> his faith is counted for righteousness.

And also in John 6:28-29:

> Then said they unto him, What shall we do, that
> we might work the works of God? Jesus answered
> and said unto them, This is the work of God, that
> ye believe on him whom he hath sent.

This is "the simplicity that is in Christ" (II Corinthians 11:3). If you still believe that Jesus Christ is your *model* rather than your *Savior* and that you can attain the same level that He did, then you would also have to:

- Have been born of a virgin (Isaiah 7:14, Matthew 1:18)
- Tell someone their whole life history without ever having met them and not be wrong (John 4:28-29)
- Raise the dead (Matthew 9:24-25)
- Raise yourself from the dead (Matthew 16:21; John 2:19-21)
- Create and uphold the material universe (Colossians 1:16-17) and specifically be *head of the church* (vs. 18), and the *King of Israel* (Acts 2:29-30, Luke 1:32)
- Come back to earth at the head of a mighty host and have every knee bow and have every tongue confess that *you are Lord* (Philippians 2:10-11)
- Most important of all, were you to truly follow Christ's example, you would die for the sins of the whole world and by your death the whole world would have redemption through *your blood*.

New Agers who see themselves as "christs" have not "tasted death for every man" nor can anyone have redemption through *their* blood. Through their meditation experiences they have been deceived by familiar spirits into believing it is their *Christ-selves* that they are in touch with.

Faith in What?

A friend of mine, who is a member of the Body of Christ, was visiting his parents. His mother, who was an elder in a prosperous suburban protestant church, asked him whether he was saving his money or not. He told her that he felt the Lord was returning soon and that saving money was not one of his prime goals.

Displeased at what she heard, his mother began to chide him for his remark. In return he asked her, "What do you believe in, Mom?"

"I have *faith*, Larry, I have *faith*," she replied.

"In *what*, Mom?"

"I have faith in my church and human nature," she proudly proclaimed.

It is sadly apparent that this woman, despite her church background, already had one foot in the New Age, as millions like her also have.

This view is backed up by research data. One source reveals:

> While religion is highly popular in America, it is to a large extent superficial; it does not change people's lives to the degree one would expect from their level of professed faith. Related to this is a "knowledge gap" between Americans' stated faith and the lack of the most basic knowledge about that faith.[1]

In the spring of 1991, New York University released a nationwide study which showed 86 percent of all Americans identified with Christianity. Yet, another study showed that only nineteen percent of Americans knew that being a Christian was having a *personal* relationship with Jesus Christ.[2] If they mean by having a personal relationship that they have believed the Gospel and now see Jesus Christ as their Lord and Savior, then these people would also be in a position to reject the New Age view of embracing your higher self through meditation. But for those who view Jesus as someone who is a benevolent religious leader who they can model themselves after, then these people would be very much open to the New Age view. There are those who consider themselves Christians but do not subscribe to Jesus as their Lord and Savior in the *personal* sense but more of one who is a super example of the Christ consciousness.

Many people have not grasped what "the gospel of your salvation" is all about—which can be summed up by the following verses:

> This is a faithful saying, and worthy of all acceptation, that Christ Jesus came into the world to save sinners; of whom I am chief. (I Timothy 1:15)

> But not as the offence, so also is the free gift. For if through the offence of one [Adam] many be dead, much more the grace of God, and the gift by grace,

> *which is by one man, Jesus Christ,* hath abounded unto
> many. (Romans 5:15, emphasis mine)

Salvation is having personal faith and trust in the *person* and
finished work (sacrifice) of the Lord Jesus Christ. We have "peace
with God" (Romans 5:1), are "forgiven" (Ephesians 5:4), and are
"reconciled" to God (II Corinthians 5:18) only by *Him*. That's
where our faith or trust is to be directed. The notion of achieving
Christ consciousness is just not compatible with being redeemed by
Christ's precious blood. The two just don't mix. Romans 5:6 says:

> For when we were yet without strength [spiritually
> impotent], in due time Christ *died* for the ungodly.

A *consciousness* can't die for anyone—only a *person* can. If you
"receive not the love of the truth," as Scripture says, your eternal
destination will be determined:

> Even him, whose coming is after the working of
> Satan with all power and signs and lying wonders,
> And with all deceivableness of unrighteousness in
> them that perish; because they received not the love
> of the truth, that they might be saved. And for this
> cause God shall send them strong delusion, that
> they should believe a lie. (II Thessalonians 2:9-11)

I would like you to really ponder the profound significance
of these verses.

God's Desire

Just what exactly is God's desire for mankind? Does He want
to send people to Hell? Does He want anyone to live eternally
without Him? Scripture is very clear about this when it says:

> The Lord is not slack concerning his promise, as
> some men count slackness; but is longsuffering to

us-ward, not willing that any should perish, but
that all should come to repentance. (II Peter 3:9)

God makes a strong plea to all people, giving them every
opportunity to receive Him. It is God's desire that none should
perish eternally. That's why he offered His Son, the Lord Jesus
Christ—the only perfect sacrifice for mankind's sin:

Therefore as by the offence of one [Adam] judgment
came upon all men to condemnation; even so by the
righteousness of one [Jesus] the free gift came upon all
men unto justification of life. (Romans 5:18)

What it comes down to is the preaching of the *higher self* versus
the preaching of the Cross. The New Age is saying that God is the
higher self in man—that God is just a meditation away.

Many people are turned off when they think Christian teaching says we are bad and worthless. *But this is not so.* It may teach
that man is bad (which is evident) but certainly not worthless.
The fact that Christ *died* for the "ungodly" to "reconcile" them
to God shows God's love toward man. In contrast to karma, the
Gospel of grace is better in that if you accept its provision, you
are complete (perfect) in Christ Jesus.

This is why Christianity is so steadfast on these issues. If
a belief system is not preaching the Cross, then it is not "the
power of God" (I Corinthians 1:18). If other ways are correct,
then Christ died in vain, His blood shed *unnecessarily*.

A Warning and a Plea

It is very true that God loves mankind, so much so He sent His
Son to save all who receive Him by faith. The Lord is very patient
with man, and as "the day of the Lord" draws nearer and nearer,
He continues beckoning humanity to Himself.

However, while God's love, mercy, and patience are very
enduring, His warnings about a great judgment coming upon

the earth are to be taken very seriously. Those who refuse to bow their knee to Jesus Christ *will* suffer severe and eternal consequences—make no mistake, that day *will* come:

> But the heavens and the earth, which are now, by the same word are kept in store, reserved unto fire against the day of judgment and perdition of ungodly men. (II Peter 3:7)

Jesus said, in referring to His return "of that day and hour knoweth no man" (Matthew 24:36). But He also said that while we will not know the exact hour and day of His return, we should be watching for the signs of the coming tribulation period. Throughout the centuries, Christians generally thought they were living in a time when Christ's return was imminent based on natural disasters, wars, upheaval, and prominent military leaders (e.g., Napoleon). But never in the history of humanity has occultism and mysticism been unleashed as it has now. The apostle Paul, in making reference to this time period, said:

> For yourselves know perfectly that the day of the Lord so cometh as a thief in the night. For when they shall say, Peace and safety; then sudden destruction cometh upon them, as travail upon a woman with child; and they shall not escape. But ye, brethren, are not in darkness, that that day should overtake you as a thief. Ye are all the children of light, and the children of the day: we are not of the night, nor of darkness. Therefore let us not sleep, as do others; but let us watch and be sober. (I Thessalonians 5:2-6)

Many think that the New Age movement is only a recent manifestation. But I believe that the words of the prophet Isaiah reveal that New Age spirituality was even around back then, although not called that. And he links this *Ancient Wisdom* in with the *end of the age* period. Isaiah issues a stern and fearsome warning:

> Stand now with thine enchantments, and with
> the multitude of thy sorceries, wherein thou hast
> laboured from thy youth, if so be thou shalt be
> able to profit, if so be thou mayest prevail. Thou
> art wearied in the multitude of thy counsels. Let
> now the astrologers, the stargazers, the monthly
> prognosticators, stand up, and save thee from these
> things that shall come upon thee. (Isaiah 47:12-13)

The next verse describes the judgment that these will be
subjected to:

> Behold, they shall be as stubble; the fire shall burn
> them; they shall not deliver themselves from the
> power of the flame. (Isaiah 47:14)

And in Revelation 9:20-21, it discloses:

> And the rest of the men which were not killed
> by these plagues yet repented not of the works of
> their hands, that they should not worship devils,
> and idols of gold, and silver, and brass, and stone,
> and of wood: which neither can see, nor hear, nor
> walk: *Neither repented they of their murders, nor of their
> sorceries.* (emphasis mine)

The Book of Revelation explains that there are those who in
the latter times "blasphemed the name of God" and "repented
not to give him [God] glory" (Revelation 16:9) and again, "repented not of their deeds" (vs. 11).

These verses that speak of sorceries portray the "mystery of
iniquity" (II Thessalonians 2:7) that is being judged during the
tribulation period because its adherents are claiming to be God,
and they refuse to give Him the glory but rather take it upon
themselves. This will be the ultimate test revealing who the *real*
God is.

This word "sorceries" used in Revelation comes from the greek word *pharmakaia*. The word is translated into four meanings.:

1) the use or the administering of drugs
2) poisoning
3) sorcery, magical arts, often found in connection with idolatry and fostered by it
4) metaphorically the deceptions and seductions of idolatry

I want you to realize the significance of this. The Bible is clear that sorcery will be a pervasive practice, to the point of being epidemic during "the day of the Lord." And this is what is now called the Ancient Wisdom by its proponents! Alice Bailey said that the Ancient Wisdom would be at the very root of her new vital world religion, which she proudly proclaimed would be universal.

Scripture is very clear that sorceries are practices that will be judged by God. And I have shown in this book, sorcery traditionally throughout the centuries has been practiced by a very small number of persons (i.e., occult or kept secret). But now we have a virtual explosion of sorcery through the various practices and pronouncements as you have now read. What I am talking about is a whole world like the psychic slave girl in Acts (see page 145).

From Genesis to Revelation, the pages are filled with God's warning to mankind when he refuses to acknowledge that the Lord is God and man is not. And throughout these pages are stories of those who mocked and scorned the warnings brought by God's messengers. The apostle Peter referred to this scenario:

> Knowing this first, that there shall come in the last days scoffers, walking after their own lusts, And saying, Where is the promise of his coming? for since the fathers fell asleep, all things continue as they were from the beginning of the creation. (II Peter 3: 3-4)

Many people today believe that it is wrong to talk about and warn of an endtime, apocolyptic time period. Rather, they say, we should spend time meditating and employing our higher powers to reach happiness and enlightenment in life. We each have a choice to make. Do we seek after this consciousness, or do we humbly call upon the living God and accept His free gift of salvation and eternal life?

If you don't already, I pray you *will* come to know the *true* Christ (*Jesus* Christ) before it is too late. I cannot emphasize enough the vital importance of understanding and believing the following verse:

> I am the door: by me if any man enter in, he shall be saved, and shall go in and out, and find pasture. (John 10:9)

By saying this, Jesus made clear that it was by *Him* and not a mystical consciousness that we are saved. Let me leave you with this. Compare these four views below. I pray you will see the difference as I did so many years ago!

> I AM GOD! This is THE most basic tenant of metaphysical spiritual understanding.[3]—A metaphysical teacher

> You are God in a physical body.. . .You are all power. . . . You are all intelligence. . . . You are the creator.[4]—*The Secret*

> [T]here is no God else beside me; a just God and a Saviour; there is none beside me. Look unto me, and be ye saved, all the ends of the earth: for I am God, and there is none else. (Isaiah 45:21-22)

> He that hath the Son [*not* higher consciousness] hath life; and he that hath not the Son of God hath not life. (I John 5:12)

GLOSSARY

Ancient Wisdom

The supposed *laws of the Universe* that, when mastered, enable one to control one's own reality. Another word for metaphysics or occultism.

Aquarius/Aquarian Age

Sign of the Zodiac represented by the water carrier, Earth Age associated with this astrological sign. (See New Age)

Alice Bailey

British-born occultist who wrote under the guidance of a *familiar* spirit and channeled nineteen books on the New Age. She also popularized the term.

Blavatsky, H.P.

Russian noblewoman who founded the Theosophical Society in 1875, to spread occultism to western society.

Centering/Centering Prayer

Another term for meditation (going deep within your "center"). A type of meditation being promoted in many mainline churches under the guise of "prayer."

Chakras

Believed by New Agers to be the seven "energy centers" in man which "open up" during the kundalini affect in the individual.

Christ Consciousness

Thought by New Agers to be the state of awareness, reached in meditation, in which one realizes that one is divine and *one with God* and thereby becoming a "Christ" or an enlightened being.

Co-Creative

The idea that since we are part of God, we can create our own reality and manifest whatever we desire; hence we are all co-creators. This would fit more with the New Age concept that God is an energy rather than a personal being.

Creative Visualization

Imaging in the mind what you want to occur during meditation and then expecting it to happen. In simple terms, you are creating your own reality.

Empowerment

One's ability to create his or her own reality.

Guru

Master of metaphysics who teaches students how to attain their optimal spiritual level.

Higher Self

Supposed God-Self within that New Agers seek to connect with through meditation. Also called the Christ-Self.

Holistic or Wholistic

Body/mind/spirit considered as an inseparable unit.

Human Potential

Term used by many in the New Age movement to promote the idea that untapped mental and spiritual resources lie within every person and these can be utilized through various altered-state exercises.

Karma

Literally means *doing* one's actions. Always linked with the concept of Reincarnation. It means if one's actions are good, one is born into better circumstances in subsequent lives; if one's actions are bad, the opposite is true. This is supposed to promote right living.

Kundalini

Powerful energy that is brought on through meditation, associated with the Chakras.

Mantra

Word or words repeated either silently or verbally to induce an altered state.

Meditation

The practice of stilling and emptying the mind by concentrating on a single point (breath, mantra, candle, etc.) so one may be able to contact spiritual entities such as the "higher self" or spirit guides.

Metaphysics

The supposed science of dealing with unseen realities (the

spiritual worlds or planes) and using these skills to empower oneself to create the desired reality.

New Age

The Age of Aquarius, supposedly the Golden Age, when man becomes aware of his power and divinity.

New Thought

Movement that tries to merge classic occult concepts with Christian terminology.

Occultism

Kept secret or hidden, the practice of metaphysics throughout history.

Psychic

A person able to obtain information through metaphysical perception.

Reiki

Spiritual energy that is channeled by one attuned to the Reiki power. Literally translated God-energy.

Reincarnation

Spiritual evolution of the soul based on one's Karma or actions.

Self-Realization

Full contact with the higher self resulting in "knowing" one's self to be *God*.

Theosophical Society

Organization founded by Helena P. Blavatsky in 1875, to spread the Ancient Wisdom (i.e., occultism) throughout western society. The forerunner of the modern New Age movement.

Transpersonal

New Age term which means "beyond the personality;" that which pertains to the higher self. Common usages include transpersonal psychology or transpersonal education.

Wicca

Popular term for modern-day witchcraft. Nature religion based on metaphysical practices.

ENDNOTES

1 / WHAT IS THE NEW AGE?

1. "The Spiritual Revolution," *Wholistic Living News* (December 1985/January 1986, Vol. 8, Issue 3), p. 15.

2. Marion Weinstein, *Positive Magic: Occult Self-Help* (Custer, WA: Phoenix Pub., Inc., 1978), p. 19.

3. Anthony J. Fisichella, *Metaphysics: The Science of Life* (St. Paul, MN: Llewellyn Publications, 1984), p. 28.

4. Marion Weinstein, *Positive Magic*, op. cit., p. 25.

5. Anthony J. Fisichella, *Metaphysics: The Science of Life*, op. cit., p. 11.

6. Celeste G. Graham, *The Layman's Guide to Enlightenment* (Phoenix, AZ: Illumination Pub., 1980), p. 13.

7. Ananda's Expanding Light, *Program Guide* (The Expanding Light retreat center, California, April-December 1991), p. 5.

8. The College of Metaphysical Studies website, "Frequently Asked Questions About Metaphysics, Spirituality and Shamanism" (http://www.cms.edu/faq.html, accessed 11/2011).

9. "Yoga, Meditation, and Healing: A Talk with Joseph Martinez," (*Holistic Health Magazine*, Winter 1986), p. 9.

10. Brother Mandus, *The Wondrous Way of Life* (London, UK: L. N. Fowler & Co. LTD, 14th Edition, 1985), p. 28.

11. Swami Rama, *Freedom From the Bondage of Karma* (Glenview, IL: Himalayan International Institute of Yoga Science and Philosophy of U.S.A., 1977), p. 66.

12. Diane Stein, *The Women's Spirituality Book* (St. Paul, MN: Llewellyn Publications, 1998), pp. 140-141.

13.Ibid., pp. 141-142.

14. John Randolph Price, *The Superbeings* (New York, NY: Ballantine Books, 1989), p. 100.

15. Barbara Marx Hubbard, *Manual for Co-Creators of the Quantum Leap* (Gainsville, FL: New Visions, 1986), pp. vi-23.

16. *Light of Mind Catalog*, Issue 17, p. 4.

17. Shirley MacLaine, *Dancing In the Light* (New York, NY: Bantam Books, 1985), p. 350.

18. Kathy Zook, "Card Readings: May Be More Than Luck of the Draw" (*The News Guard*, Lincoln City, Oregon, February 4, 1987), Section C, p. 1.

19. Celeste G. Graham, *The Layman's Guide to Enlightenment*, op. cit., p. 55.

2/THE ADVENT OF THE "ANCIENT WISDOM"

1. George Trevelyan, *A Vision of the Aquarian Age* (Walpole, NH: Stillpoint Publishing, 1984), p. 161, book also online at http://www.sirgeorgetrevelyan.org.uk/books/thtbk-VAA14.html, accessed 11/2011.

2. Kathy Juline, "Awakening to Your Life's Purpose" (*Science of Mind*, October 2006), pp. 16-18.

3. Geoffrey Parrinder, *World Religions from Ancient History to the Present* (New York, NY: Facts on File Publications, 1983), p. 155.

4. Charles J. Ryan, *What is Theosophy? A General View of Occult Doctrine* (San Diego, CA: Point Loma Publications, Inc., revised edition, 1975), p. 16.

5. Colin Wilson and John Grant, *The Directory of Possibilities* (New York, NY: The Rutledge Press, 1981), p. 50.

6. Harold Balyoz, *Three Remarkable Women* (Flagstaff, AZ: Atlas Publishers, 1986), p. 207.

7. Ibid., p. 210.

8. Ibid., p. 213.

9. Ibid., p. 195.

10. Alice A. Bailey, *The Reappearance of the Christ* (New York, NY: Lucis Publishing. Co., 1962, fourth printing), pp. 187-188.

11. Ibid.

12. Ken Cary, *The Starseed Transmissions* (Kansas City, MO: UniSun Pub., fourth printing, 1985), pp. 3-4.

13. Ibid., pp. 31-32.

14. Bryant Reeve, *The Advent of the Cosmic Viewpoint* (Amherst, WI: Amherst Press, 1965), p. 260.

15. Matthias Horx, "Eine Bewegung Hebt Ab" (A movement takes off) (*Tempo Magazine*, December 12, 1986), pp. 45-46.

16. Glastonbury Festival website (http://www.glastonburyfestivals. co.uk, accessed 11/2011).

17. Peter Spink, *Spiritual Man in a New Age* (London, UK: Darton, Longman and Todd, Ltd., 1980), p. 45.

18. Alla Svirinskaya, *Energy Secrets* (Carlsbad, CA: Hay House, Inc., 2005), from Foreword.

19. Gale Warner and Michael Shuman, *Citizen Diplomats* (New York, NY: Continuum International Publishing Group), pp. 195-196, 200.

20. Galina Dutkina with Catherine Fitzpatrick (translator), *Moscow Days: Life and Hard Times in the New Russia* (New York, NY: Kodansha America, Inc., 1996), pp. 203-204.

21. "Falun Gong: a brief but turbulent history" (*Cnn.com/World*, July 24, 2002, http://edition.cnn.com/2002/WORLD/asiapcf/ east/07/24/china.fg.overview, accessed 11/2011.)

22. Bryant Reeve, *The Advent of the Cosmic Viewpoint*, op. cit., p. 260.

23. "Lazaris," Concept: Synergy, Promotional Flyer (Fairfax, CA).

24. David Spangler, *Emergence: The Rebirth of the Sacred* (New York, NY: Dell Publishing Company, 1984), p. 67.

25. Talk by Ken Carey at Whole Life Expo (Los Angeles: February, 1987).

26. Kathleen Vande Kieft, *Innersource: Channeling Your Unlimited Self* (New York, NY: Ballantine Books, 1989), p. 38.

27. J. L. Simmons, *The Emerging New Age* (Santa Fe, NM: Bear and Co., 1990), p. 211.

28. Ibid., p. 13.

29. James A. Herrick, *The Making of the New Spirituality* (Downers Grove, IL: InterVarsity Press, 2003), p. 16.

30. Nancy Gibbs, "An In-Depth View of America by the Numbers" (*Time* magazine, October 22, 2006), Section: "What We Believe."

3/ON THE PATH

1. Alice Bailey, *Problems of Humanity* (New York, NY: Lucis Publishing Co., Chapter VI, "The Problem of International Unity", 1993 edition), p. 178, book is also online at http://web. archive.org/web/20070219033404/http://laluni.helloyou.ws/ netnews/bk/problems/toc.html, accessed 11/2011.

2. Robert C. Fuller, *Spiritual But Not Religious* (New York, NY: Oxford University Press, Inc., 2001), p. 99.

3. "New Thought: The Religion of Healthy Mindedness" (*New Thought* magazine, Spring 1987), p. 10.

4. An interview with George Norman Hynd (*Connections*, Co. 2, No. 11, November 1982), p. 6.

5. Neal Vahle, *The Unity Movement: Its Evolution and Spiritual Teachings* (Radnor, PA: Templeton Foundation Press, 2002, citing Norman Vincent Peale), p. 423.

6. Ibid.

7. Ibid., Vahle citing Charles Braden.

8. Marcus Bach, *The Unity Way* (Unity Village, MO: Unity School of Christianity, 1982), p. 267.

9. Ibid., p. 104.

10. Robert Schuller, *Prayer: My Soul's Adventure with God* (Nashville, TN: Thomas Nelson, 1995), pp. 141, 151.

11. Lacy Ketzner, "Yoga: Not just for mumbo-jumbo freaks anymore!" (*The Yale Herald* journal, January 16, 2004 Vol. XXXVII, No. 1 http://web.archive.org/web/20060315005542/http://www. yaleherald.com/article.php?Article=2763, accessed 11/2011).

12. Starhawk, *The Spiral Dance: A Rebirth of the Ancient Religion of the Great Goddess* (San Francisco, CA: HarperSanFrancisco, 1999, Special 20th Anniversary edition), p. 66.

13. Statistics taken from Llewellyn Publishing Company, http://www.llewellyn.com.

14. Arther Egendorf, *Healing from the War: Trauma and Transformation After Vietnam* (Boston, MA: Shambhala Publications., 1985), p. 270.

15. Landmark Forum website, http://www.landmarkeducation. com/about_landmark_education.jsp, accessed 11/2011.

16. Silva Method website, http://www.silvamethod.com/

about/default.aspx, accessed 11/2011.

17. Berkeley Psychic Institute, information from website, http://web.archive.org/web/20071010034020/http://www.berkeleypsychic.com/quicktour.htm, accessed 11/2011.

18. Ibid.

19. Wisdom University, information from website, https://www.wisdomuniversity.org/aboutus.html, accessed 11/2011.

20. Joel Stein, "Just Say Om" (*Time* magazine, July 27, 2003).

21. Ken Wilber, *The Marriage of Sense and Soul* (New York, NY: Random House, First Broadway Books paperback edition, 1999), back cover.

22. Warren Smith, *Reinventing Jesus Christ* (Magalia, CA: Mountain Stream Press, updated, online edition, chapter 3 at http://web.archive.org/web/20090123035356/http://reinventingjesuschrist.com/updates/3.html, accessed 11/2011), citing the Humanity's Team Leadership Gathering, Portland, Oregon, June 27-July 1, 2003: "The Care and Feeding of the Press." Transcribed from audiotape.

23. Neale Donald Walsch, *Friendship with God* (New York, NY: The Berkeley Publishing Group, Berkeley's trade paperback edition, 2002), pp. 295, 296.

24. Ibid., p. 373.

25. Warren Smith, *Reinventing Jesus Christ* (Ravenna, OH: Conscience Press, printed edition, 2002) p. 11. (now titled False Christ Coming; see: http://www.lighthousetrails.com/mm5/merchant.mvc?Screen=PROD&Store_Code=LTP&Product_Code=FCC&Category_Code=NA.

26. Laura Tuma, "Walter Cronkite, 'The most trusted man in America'" (University of Texas at Austin, Utopia, Texas Tribute, Spring 1997, http://replay.web.archive.org/20070305083733/http://utopia.utexas.edu/articles/tribute/cronkite.html).

27. See the Campaign to Establish a U.S. Department of Peace website: http://www.thepeacealliance.org.

4/THE NEW AGE IN BUSINESS

1. E. Armstrong, "Bottom-Line Intuition" (*New Age Journal* , December 1985), p. 32.

2. "What's New in the New Age?" (*Training Magazine*, September 1987), p. 25.

3. Interview with Marilyn Ferguson (*Science of Mind* magazine, May 1983), pp. 11-12.

4. "From Burnout to Balance," Interview with Dennis Jaffe, Ph.D., (*Science of Mind* magazine, June 1985), pp. 88-89.

5. Michael Ray and Rochelle Meyers, *Creativity in Business* (Garden City, New York, NY: Doubleday and Company, Inc., 1986), front cover.

6. Ibid., back cover.

7. Ibid., back flap.

8. Ibid., pp. 36-37.

9. Ibid., p. 142.

10. Ibid., p. 154.

11. T. Harv Eker, author of *Secrets of the Millionare Mind*; quote taken from Eker's Peak Potentials Training website, http://www.peakpotentials.com/new, accessed 11/2011.

12. Marci McDonald, "Shush. The Guy in the Cubicle is Meditating: Spirituality is the latest corporate buzzword" (*U.S. News & World Report*, May 3, 1999), p. 46.

13. Ibid.

14. Kathy Juline, "Wellness Works: A New Lifestyle for a New World," Interview with Elaine Willis, Ph.D. (*Science of Mind* magazine, June 1990), p. 25.

15. Ibid., pp. 19-20.

16. Ibid.

17. Interview with James Fadiman (*Science of Mind* magazine, June 1988), p. 77.

18. "Changing the Game in Business," Interview with Larry Wilson (*Science of Mind* magazine, February 1987), p. 10.

19. Ibid., p. 14.

20. Willis Harman, "The New Age of Consciousness" (*Guide to New Age Living*, 1989), pp. 18, 20.

21. "Disciples of the New Age," (*International Management* magazine, March, 1991), p. 45.

22. Larry Wilson Interview, op. cit., p. 31.

23. 2007 *Shift Report: Evidence of a World Transforming Journal*

(Petaluma, CA: Institute of Noetic Sciences, March-May 2007, No. 14, 2007), p. 55.

5/NEW AGE IN EDUCATION

1. Marilyn Ferguson, *The Aquarian Conspiracy* (Los Angeles: J.P. Tarcher, Inc., 1980), p. 280.

2. Ibid., p. 281.

3. Ronald Miller, "Education In The New Age," Interview with Jack Canfield, Ph.D. (*Science of Mind* magazine, December 1981), p. 11.

4. Promotional Flyer, Self-Esteem Seminars, Pacific Palisades, California

5. Ibid.

6. Ronald Miller, "Education in the New Age," op. cit., p. 108.

7. Gay Hendricks and Russell Wills, *The Centering Book* (Englewood Cliffs, NJ: Prentice-Hall, Inc., 1975), pp. 169, 171.

8. Promotional flyer by Storma Swanson at Styles for Relaxation store in Portland, Oregon.

9. Storma Swanson, *Attuning to inner Guidance* (Beaverton, OR: Seabreeze Press, 1982), p. 3.

10. Ibid., p. 16.

11. Rachel Kessler, *The Soul of Education* (Alexandria, VA: Association for Supervision and Curriculum Development, 2000), Introduction, p. ix.

12. Ibid., p. 117.

13. Ibid., pp. 133, 134.

14. Ibid., p. 134, citing J. W. Peterson, *The Secret Life of Kids: An Exploration into their Psychic Senses* (Theosophical Publishing House), p. 210.

15. American Medical Association House of Delegates, "Depression and Suicide on College Campuses" (Resolution: 425, A-05).

16. "Students Seek Quiet Within" (*The Oregonian*, December 7, 2005).

17. "Meditation Workshop" at Santa Fe Community College, http://admin.sfcc.edu/~pbreslin/OM, (no longer online).

18. Information taken from Mark Blanchard's website, http://

web.archive.org/web/20061230212533/http://www.progressive-
poweryoga.com/, accessed 11/2011.

19. Ibid.

20. Patricia Leigh Brown, "Latest Way to Cut Grade School
Stress: Yoga" (*New York Times*, March 24, 2002).

21. *The Learning Annex*, a brochure (Seattle Center, October
1987), pp. 7, 11.

22. The Learning Annex, information from the website,
http://web.archive.org/web/20070210005037/http://www.
learningannex.com, accessed 02/2007.

23. Ezra Bowen, "Bargains in Short-Order Courses" (*Time* magazine, December 15, 1986).

6/HOLISTIC HEALING AND ALTERNATIVE HEALTH

1. "Healing Hands," *New Woman Magazine* (March 1986).

2. Dennis Livingston, "Balancing Body, Mind, and Spirit"
(*Guide to New Age Living*, 1988), p. 17.

3. Robert Hass and Cher, *Forever Fit* (New York, NY: Bantam
Books, 1991), p. 165.

4. Joy Gardner-Gordon, *Pocket Guide to Chakras* (Freedom, CA:
The Crossing Press, 1998), p. 13.

5. "Healing Hands," op. cit., p. 78.

6. Joyce Morris, "The Reiki Touch" (*The Movement Newspaper*,
October 1985).

7. Barbara Ray, Ph.D., *The Reiki Factor* (Smithtown, NY:
Exposition Press, 1983), p. 63.

8. "Vincent J. Barra Psychic Healer Transmits Reiki Energy"
(*Meditation Magazine*, Summer 1991), p. 31.

9. William Lee Rand, "Keeping Reiki Free" (*Reiki News Magazine*,
Spring 2005), p. 37

10. Mari Hall, "Reiki and the Adventure of My Life" (*Reiki News
Magazine*, Summer 2006), p. 14.

11. Paula Horan, *Empowerment Through Reiki* (Wilmot, WI:
Lotus Light Publications, 1990), p. 9.

12. Bodo J. Baginski and Shalila Sharamon, *Reiki Universal Life*

Energy (Mendocino, CA: Life Rhythm, 1988), pp. 33, 49-50.

13. "Sharings" (*The Reiki Journal*, Vol. VI, No. 4, October/December 1986), p. 17.

14. William Lee Rand, "The Nature of Reiki Energy" (*The Reiki News*, Autumn 2000, p. 5.

15. *The Reiki News*, Spring 2006, p. 43.

16. D. Scott Rogo, "The Potentials of Therapeutic Touch," Interview with Janet F. Quinn, Ph.D., R.N. (*Science of Mind*, May 1988), p. 14.

17. Ibid., p. 83.

18. Ibid., pp. 83-84.

19. Ibid., p. 87.

20. Phyllis Galde, *The Truth About Crystal Healing* (St. Paul, MN: Llewellyn Publications, 1987), p. 9.

21. *Magical Blend Magazine*, Issue 14, p. 14.

22. Barbara Ann Brennan, *Hands of Light* (New York, NY: Bantam Books, 1987), p. 171.

23. Ibid., p. 187.

24. Ibid., p. 182.

25. Ibid.

26. *USA Weekend Sunday Supplement*, July 24-26, 1987, p. 12.

27. Jach Pursel, "Introduction from the Sacred Journey: You and Your Higher Self," taken from Jach Pursel's website, http://www.lazaris.com/publibrary/pubjach.cfm, accessed 11/2011.

28. *Mark Vaz*, "The Many Faces of Keven Ryerson" (*Yoga Journal*, July/August 1986), p. 28.

29. "Two Billion People for Peace," Interview with John Randolph Price (*Science of Mind*, Aug. 1989), p. 24.

30. Laurie Cabot, *Power of the Witch* (New York, NY: Bantam Doubleday Dell Publishing, 1989), p. 173.

31. Kathleen Vande Kieft, *Innersource: Channeling Your Unlimited Self* (New York, NY: Ballantine Books, third printing, 1989), p. 114.

32. Zolar, *Zolar's Book of the Spirits* (New York, NY: Prentice Hall Press, 1987), p. 227.

33. Betty Bethards, *Way to Awareness: A Technique of Concentration and Meditation* (Novato, CA: Inner Light Foundation, 1987), p. 23.

34. "The Pundit of Transpersonal Psychology" (*Yoga Journal*, September/October 1987), p. 43.

35. Marty Kaplan, "Ambushed by Spirituality" (*Time* magazine, June 24, 1996, http://www.time.com/time/magazine/article/0,9171,984754,00.html, accessed 11/2011).

36. Ibid.

37. Andrea Honebrick, "Meditation: Hazardous to your health?" (*Utne Reader*, March/April 1994), citing Nathaniel Mead (*Natural Health* November/December 1993, taken from the Transcendental Meditation Ex-Members Support Group, TM-EX Newsletter at http://minet.org/news94sm.dtp.0.html, accessed 11/2011).

38. Mayo Foundation for Medical Education and Research, *Mayo Clinic Book of Alternative Medicine* (Time, Inc., Home Entertainment Books, 2007), p. 90.

7/NEW AGE IN ARTS AND MEDIA

1. Michelle Roberts "Wellness and Spirituality" (*The Oregonian* newspaper in the Living: Wellness/Spirituality section, June 7, 2006), p. C1, C3.

2. Ibid.

3. Information taken from *Willamette Week Online*, http://www.wweek.com.

4. "Four Basic Spiritual Practices to Increase Positive Energy" (*Spirituality & Health*, May/June 2004).

5. Robert C. Fuller, *Spiritual But Not Religious*, op. cit., p. 155.

6. Judith Rosen, "Casting a Wider Spell" (*Publishers Weekly*, September 1, 2003).

7. J. K. Rowling, *Harry Potter and the Prisoner of Azkaban* (London, UK: Bloomsbury Publishing, 1999), p. 297.

8. Raymond Buckland, *Buckland's Complete Book of Witchcraft* (St. Paul, MN: Llewellyn Publications, fourth printing, 1987), p. 80.

9. J. K. Rowling, *Harry Potter and the Prisoner of Azkaban*, op. cit., term used in book.

10. Marielena Zuniga, "The Higher Power of Oprah Winfrey" (*Science of Mind*, September 2006), p. 80.

11. Ibid., 84.

12. Ibid.

13. Ibid., p. 82.

14. Ibid., p. 80.

15. Taken from the Sterling International Speakers Bureau website, http://web.archive.org/web/20060618004411/http://www.sterlingspeakers.com/dyer.htm, accessed 11/2011.

16. Kathy Juline, "Everyday Miracles, An Interview with Dr. Wayne Dyer (*Science of Mind* magazine, January 1993), p. 30.

17. Ibid., p. 35.

18. Barbara Marx Hubbard, *The Revelation* (Mill Valley, CA: Natarj Publishing, 1995), p. 243.

19. Information taken from the New Dimensions Media website, http://web.archive.org/web/20080218035918/http://www.newdimensions.org/program.php?id=2531, accessed 11/2011.

20. Chris Lydgate, "What the #$*! is Ramtha" (*Willamette Week*, December 22, 2004, http://www.rickross.com/reference/ramtha/ramtha15.html, accessed 11/2011).

21. Information taken from the Celestine Prophecy website, http://thecelestineprophecymovie.com/about.php, accessed 11/2011.

22. *Empire Strikes Back* movie, episode V of the Star Wars series.   For more information: http://web.archive.org/web/20040211065601/http://www.starwars.com/episode-v/, accessed 11/2011.

23. Ibid.

24. Jess Cagle, "So What's the Deal with Leia's Hair?" (*Time* magazine, April 29, 2002).

25. See http://www.witchvox.com.

26. Rhonda Byrne, *The Secret* (New York, NY: Atria Books, 2006), p. 164.

27. Rhonda Byrne, *The Secret* (New York, NY: Atria Books and Hillsboro, OR: Beyond Words Publishing, First Atria Books/Beyond Words hardcover edition, 2006), Acknowledgements, p. xv.

28. From Jerry and Esther Hicks website, http://www.abrahamhicks.com/about_us.php, accessed 11/2011.

29. Ronda Byrne, *The Secret*, op. cit., p. 183.

30. Thomas Herold, "The Secret Boosts Sales of Other Inspira-

tional Books" (*Dream Manifesto*, February 22, 2007, http://www. dreammanifesto.com/the-secret-boosts-sales-of-other-inspirational-books.html, accessed 11/2011).

31. Jack Canfield, *The Success Principles* (New York, NY: Harper-Collins, 2005), pp. 316, 317.

32. See video series on Oprah and *The Secret*, http://video.google. com.videoplay?docid=6970591609350288402&q=oprah+the+secr et, (no longer online).

8 / NEW AGE IN SELF-HELP

1. Quoted from Creative Growth website at http://www.creativeg-rowth.com/johnbio.htm, accessed 11/2011.

2. John Bradshaw, *Bradshaw on the Family* (Pompono Beach, FL: Health Communications, 1988), p. 235.

3. John Bradshaw, *Healing the Shame That Binds You* (Deerfield Beach, FL: Health Communications, 1988), p. 222.

4. John Bradshaw, *Bradshaw on the Family*, op. cit., p. 229.

5. John Bradshaw, *Healing the Shame*, op. cit., p. 223.

6. Melody Beattie, *The Co-dependent's Guide to the Twelve Steps* (New York, NY: Simon & Schuster, First Fireside edition, 1992), pp. 179-180.

7. Ibid., pp. 262-265.

8. Ibid., pp. 187-188.

9. Robin Norwood, *Women Who Love too Much* (New York, NY: Pocket Books, First Pocket Books printing, 1986), p. 236.

10. Ibid.

11. Ibid., in back of book under "Suggested Reading," p. 295.

12. Alexandra Stoddard, *You are Your Choices* (New York, NY: Harper/Collins, 2006), p. 157.

13. Ibid.

14. Ibid., p. 158.

15. D. Scott Rogo, "Music, Stress, and Your Health" Interview with Steven Halpern (*Science of Mind* magazine, February 1989), p. 14.

16. Ibid.

17. Ibid., p. 15.

18. Ibid., p. 72.

19. Joy Lake Seminar Center, 1988 catalog, p. 43.

20. *Reflections Resource Directory*, Portland, Oregon, Fall 1986, p. 16.

21. "Meeting Your Inner Guide," article in publication put out by local New Age bookstore.

22. Ibid.

23. David Quigley, *Alchemical Hypnotheray: A new dimension in therapeutic technology* (Alchemical Hypnotherapy Institute, Santa Rosa, California, March 1993).

24. Ibid.

25. Wahkeena Sitka Tidepool Ripple, "Can Sex Work Be Shamanic?" (*Alternatives: A magazine for the emerging culture*, Winter 06-07), p. 17.

26. Ibid.

27. Ibid.

28. Ibid.

29. Ibid., p. 14.

9 / NEW AGE IN RELIGION

1. Thomas Keating, Basil Pennington, and Thomas Clarke, *Finding Grace at the Center* (Petersham, MA: St. Bede's Publications, Fourth Revised edition, 1985), p. 5.

2. Ibid., p. 6.

3. Basil Pennington, *Centering Prayer* (Garden City, NY: Image Books, Image Book edition, 1982), p. 163.

4. Anthony de Mello, S. J., *Sadhana: A Way to God* (India: X. Diaz del Rio, S.J., Gujarat Sahitya Prakash, Anand, Gujarat, 5th Edition, Third printing, 1980), inside front cover.

5. Ibid., p. 3.

6. Ibid., p. 9.

7. Ibid.

8. Ibid., p. 15

9. William Johnson, *The Mystic Way* (London, UK: HarperCollins, 1993), the Foreword.

10. Wake Up to Life flyer (St. Louis, Missouri: We and God

Spirituality Center), p. 2.

11. Harvey D. Egan, S. J. (The Catholic Theological Society of America, *Proceedings*, 1980, p. 104), cited on back cover of *Sadhana: A Way to God* by Anthony de Mello.

12. Benjamin Walker, *The Hindu World* (New York, NY: Frederick A. Praeger Pub., Vol. 11, M-2, 1968), p. 394.

13. James Finley, Michael Pennock, *Your Faith and You* (Notre Dame MD: Ave Maria Press, 1978), p. 205.

14. Richard Chilson, *Full Christianity* (Mahwah, NJ: Paulist Press, 1985).

15. Ibid., p. 136.

16. David R. Griffen, *San Francisco Sunday Punch*, March 8, 1987.

17. James Fadiman (*Science of Mind*, June 1988), p. 77.

18. Richard E. Geis' personal journal, "The Naked Id."

19. "New Age Isn't New to Salem" (*Statesman Journal* newspaper article, Salem, Oregon, March 9, 1991), p. 2-A.

20. Marcus Borg, *The God We Never Knew* (New York, NY: Harper Collins, First HarperCollins Paperback edition, 1998), pp. 25, 29.

21. Ibid.

22. Ibid.

23. M. Scott Peck, M.D., *The Road Less Traveled* (New York, NY: Simon and Schuster, Inc., 1978), p. 270.

24. Charles Leerhsen, "Peck's Path to Inner Peace" (*Newsweek*, November 18, 1985), p.79.

25. From the Kabbalah Centre website, http://blog.kabbalah.com/michael/bio/en, (no longer online)

26. Ibid.

27. Melinda Ribner, *New Age Judaism: Ancient Wisdom for the Modern World* (Deerfield Beach, FL: Simcha Press, 2000), p. 49.

28. Ibid.

29. Ken Carey, *The Starseed Transmissions*, op. cit., p. 33.

30. David Spangler, *Emergence: The Rebirth of the Sacred*, op. cit., p. 112.

31. M. Basil Pennington O.C.S.D., *Centered Living the Way of Centering Prayer* (Liguori, MO: Liguori Publications, Revised edition,

1999), pp. 198, 200.

32. Matthew Fox, *The Coming of the Cosmic Christ* (New York, NY: HarperCollins, 1988), p. 65.

33. Ibid.

34. From the Sophia Institute website, http://web.archive.org/web/20070308123436/http://www.studiophoebepemberhouse.com/OurWork.aspx, accessed 11/2011.

35. Sue Monk Kidd, *The Dance of the Dissident Daughter* (New York, NY: HarperCollins, First HarperCollins Paperback edition, 2002), p. 160.

36. Sue Monk Kidd, *First Light* (Carmel, NY: Guideposts Books, 2006) pp. 96, 98.

10/Is the New Age Wrong?

1. Shakti Gawain, *Creative Visualization* (San Rafael, CA: Whatever Publishing, 1978), p. 14.

2. Ibid., p. 56.

3. Ibid., p. 91.

4. Ibid., p. 93.

5. James S. Gordon, *The Golden Guru* (Lexington, MN: The Stephen Greene Press, 1988), p. 8.

6. Donald Yott, *Man and Metaphysics* (New York, NY: Sam Weiser, Inc., 1980), p. 103.

7. Shakti Gawain, *Creative Visualization*, op. cit., p. 15.

8. David Spangler, *Reflections on the Christ* (Findhorn Foundation, second edition, 1978), p. 36.

9. Ibid., p. 41.

10. Jennifer Thebodeau, "What Happens During a Reiki Treatment?" (Mountain Sky Reiki, Osaka, Japan,http://www.mountainskyreiki.com/reikitreatments.htm, accessed 11/2011).

11. Barbara Ray, Ph.D., *The Reiki Factor* (Smithtown, NY: Exposition Press, Inc., 1983), p. 12.

12. David Eastman, "Kundalini Demystified" (*Yoga Journal*, September/October 1985), p. 43.

13. "Baba Beleaguered" (*Yoga Journal*, July/August 1985), p. 30, (reprinted from *CoEvolution Quarterly* Winter 1983).

14. Stan Trout, excerpts from an open letter (*Yoga Journal*, July/ August 1985), p. 30.

11/THE END OF THE AGE?

1. Charles Fillmore, *Metaphysical Bible Dictionary* (Unity Village, MO: Unity School of Christianity).

2. Donald H. Yott, *Man and Metaphysics*, op. cit., p. 73.

3. John White, "Jesus, Evolution, and the Future of Humanity" (*Science of Mind* magazine, September 1981), p. 15.

4. John Davis and Naomi Rice, *Messiah and the Second Coming* (Wyoming, MI: Coptic Press, 1982), p. 49.

5. John White (*Science of Mind* magazine, October 1981), pp. 40-42.

6. John White, "Jesus, Evolution, and the Future of Humanity," op. cit, p. 15.

7. Armand Biteaux, *The New Consciousness* (Willits, CA: Oliver Press, 1975), p. 128.

8. Gregory Barrette, "The Christ is Now" (*Science of Mind*, March 1989), p. 17.

9. *Life Times*, Vol. 1, No.3, p. 91.

10. John Randolph Price, *The Planetary Commission* (Austin, TX: Quaratus Books, 1984), pp. 143, 145.

11. Anne P. and Peter V. Meyer, *Being a Christ* (San Diego: Dawning Pub., 1975), p. 49.

12. John Baughman, *The New Age* (Self-Published, 1977), p. 5.

13. John Randolph Price, *The Planetary Commission*, op. cit. p. 98.

14. Simons Roof, *About the Aquarian Age* (The Mountain School of Esoteric Studies), p. 7.

15. Donald H. Yott, *Man and Metaphysics*, op. cit., p. 74.

16. *Life Times*, Vol. 1, No. 3, p. 90.

17. John Davis and Naomi Rice, *Messiah and the Second Coming*, op. cit., p. 150.

18. James S. Gordon, *The Golden Guru: The Strange Journey of Bhagwan Shree Rajneesh* (Lexington, MA: The Stephen Greene Press, 1988), p. 236.

19. Alice A. Bailey, *The Reappearance of the Christ* (Albany, NY:

Fort Orange Press, fourth printing, 1962), p. 124.

20. Ron Roth, Ph.D., *Holy Spirit for Healing* (Carlsbad, CA: Hay House, Inc., 2001), p. 23.

21. Ibid., p. 24.

22. Agnes Sanford, *The Healing Light* (New York, NY: Ballantine Books/Random House, Revised edition, 1972), p. 3.

23. Ibid., pp. 3-4.

24. Ibid., p. 5.

25. Ibid., pp. 167, 25.

26. Ibid., pp. 27, 61.

27. Ibid., p. 21.

28. Agnes Sanford, *Sealed Orders* (Plainfield, NJ: Logos International, 1972), pp. 190, 103.

29. Martin A. Larson, *New Thought Religion* (New York, NY: Philosophical Library, 1987, Revised and Updated edition), pp. 180-181.

30. Marjorie L. Rand, "Healing: A Gift That Awakens" (*The Whole Person*, June 1988), p. 40.

31. Alice Bailey, *The Reappearance of the Christ*, op. cit., p. 124.

32. Ibid., p. 121.

33. Donald Yott, *Man and Metaphysics*, op. cit., p. 58.

34. John Davis and Naomi Rice, *Messiah and the Second Coming*, op. cit., p. 152.

35. John White, "The Second Coming" (*New Frontier Magazine*, December 1987), p. 45.

36. Alice Bailey, *The Externalization of the Hierarchy* (http://web.archive.org/web/20060225031310/http://laluni.helloyou.ws/netnews/bk/externalisation/exte1119.html, accessed 11/2011), Section II - The General World Picture.

37. Warren Smith, *Reinventing Jesus Christ*, printed edition, op. cit., p. 16, citing Barbara Marx Hubbard, *Conscious Evolution: Awakening the Power of Our Social Potential* (Novato, CA: New World Library, 1998), pp. 240, 267.

38. Ibid., p. 19, Smith citing Marx Hubbard from *The Revelation* (Novato, CA: Nataraj Publishing, 1995), p. 233.

39. Neale Donald Walsch, *Conversations with God, Book 2* (Charlottesville, VA: Hampton Road Publishing Company, Inc., 1997), p. 56.

40. Ibid., p. 40.

41. Ibid., p. 36.

42. Rhonda Byrne, *The Secret*, op. cit., p. 197.

43. Geoffrey A. Barborka, *Glossary of Sanskrit Terms* (Buena Park, CA: Stockton Trade Press, Point Loma Publications, 1972), p. 64.

44. Zachary E Lansdowne, Ph. D., *The Chakras and Esoteric Healing* (York Beach, ME: Samuel Weiser, Inc., First Indian edition: Delhi, 1993), p. 114.

45. David Spangler, *Emergence: The Rebirth of the Sacred* (New York, NY: Dell Publishing Company, 1984), p. 159.

46. Geoffrey A. Barborka, op. cit., p. 15.

47. Alice Bailey, *From Intellect to Intuition* (Lucis Trust, Fifth Paperback edition, 13th printing, 1987), p. 61.

48. *Reiki News Magazine*, Spring 2004, p. 12.

12/SALVATION AND THE NEW AGE

1. George Gallup, Jr. and Jim Castelli, *The People's Religion* (New York, NY: MacMillan Pub., 1989), p. 21.

2. George Barna, *The Frog in the Kettle* (Ventura, CA: Regal Books, 1990), p. 114.

3. "I AM," Communicated through Kathy Wilson (*The Light of Olympia Newspaper* Vol. 1, Number 8, August 1988), p. 7.

4. Rhonda Byrne, *The Secret, op. cit., p. 164.*

INDEX

A

B

C

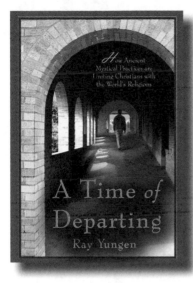

A Time of Departing
by Ray Yungen

A spirituality that has infiltrated much of the church today. Exposes the subtle strategies to compromise the Gospel message with Eastern mystical practices cloaked under evangelical terminology and wrappings.—2nd Edition, 248 pages, $12.95, softbound

Topics include:

- Contemplative Prayer
- Yoga
- Labyrinths
- Spiritual Directors
- Reiki
- Desert Fathers
- Spiritual Formation
- Spiritual Disciplines
- Purpose Driven and the Emerging Church

Ray Yungen, author, speaker, and research analyst has studied religious movements for nearly thirty years. His exuberance for life and his love for Jesus Christ and for people are evident in his writing. Mr. Yungen resides in the Willamette Valley, Oregon. He is available for speaking for radio, conferences, college classes, and other venues.

Things We Couldn't Say
by Diet Eman

The true story of Diet Eman, a young Christian woman who joined the resistance movement in the Netherlands during WWII. Together with her fiancé and other Dutch men and women, "Group Hein" risked their lives to save the lives of Jews who were in danger of becoming victims of Hitler's "final solution." Biography/Holocaust, 352 pages, $14.95, softbound, photos

Trapped in Hitler's Hell
by Anita Dittman
with Jan Markell

Anita Dittman was just a little girl when the winds of Hitler and Nazism began to blow through Germany. By the time she was twelve, the war had begun.

Abandoned by her father when he realized the price of being associated with a Jewish wife and family, Anita and her mother were ultimately left to fend for themselves. Anita's teenage years were spent desperately fighting for survival yet learning to trust in the One she discovered would never leave her. 192 pages, $12.95, softbound, photos

Laughter Calls Me
by Catherine Brown

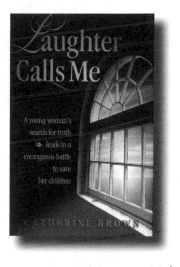

The true story of a young woman who discovers her children have become victims of child pornography. An edge of your seat, hard-to-put-down book. From a hitchhiking hippie of the seventies to a young Christian mom who must flee the country and go into hiding to protect her children, you will embark with her on a most unforgettable journey. Catherine Brown is the author's pen name, and this special 2nd edition has family photos and drawings. This is the biography of the co-founder of Lighthouse Trails Publishing.—160 pages $12.95, softbound, photos

The Color of Pain
by Gregory Reid

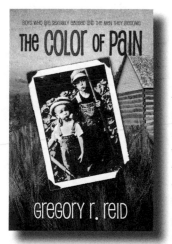

One in every six boys is sexually abused. That's just the ones who eventually tell their secret. The Color of Pain speaks to the professionals, pastors, and loved ones as well as to the boys and men who were abused. And who better to write a book like this than one of the victims who has lived the pain and later experienced the healing through Christ. The Color of Pain is a combination of some of the facts that most don't think about and some of the pain that most won't talk about. Whether you are one of the abused or someone who knows someone abused, this book is a moving and necessary read. 114 pages, $10.95, softbound

The Other Side of the River

by Kevin Reeves

When mystical experiences and strange doctrines overtake his church, one man risks all to find the truth ... a true story

A compelling and deeply personal account of a young man's spiritual plunge into a movement called "the River," which claims to be spreading the kingdom of God through signs and wonders. Sometimes referred to as the River revival, the Third Wave or the Latter Rain, this movement is marked by bizarre manifestations, false prophecies and esoteric revelations. Warnings of divine retribution keep many adherents in bondage, afraid to speak out or even question those things they are taught and are witness to.

For Kevin Reeves, the determination to rescue his family came to the forefront. Even if the cost was high and even if he had to stand alone, his journey back into the freedom and simplicity of the Gospel of Jesus Christ would be worth the price.—232 pages $12.95, softbound

Topics this book addresses:
- Word Faith movement
- Holy Laughter
- "Slain" in the Spirit practice
- Emphasis on humanity of Jesus over His Deity
- Gifts & Calling for the unbeliever?
- Experience versus Scripture
- Repetitive chanting & singing
- Paradigm shift
- Questionable worship practices

Faith Undone
by Roger Oakland

The emerging church—a new reformation or an endtime deception

Is the emerging church movement just another passing fad, a more contemporary approach to church, or a bunch of disillusioned young people looking for answers? In actuality, it is much broader than this and is influencing Christianity to a significant degree. Grounded in a centuries-old mystical approach, this movement is powerful, yet highly deceptive, and it draws its energy from practices and experiences that are foreign to traditional evangelical Christianity. The path the emerging church is taking is leading right to an interfaith perspective that has prophetically profound ramifications.—264 pages, $12.95, softbound

Another Jesus
by Roger Oakland

Many Christians think that the Christian tradition of communion is the same as the Catholic tradition of the Eucharist. But this is not so. The Eucharist (i.e., Transubstantiation), is a Catholic term for communion when the bread and the wine actually become the very body and blood of Jesus Christ, thus when taken the partaker supposedly experiences the presence of God. These transformed elements are placed in what is called a monstrance and can then be worshipped as if worshipping God Himself. The implications are tied in with salvation.—192 pages, $12.95, softbound

Other Products Available at Lighthouse Trails Publishing

BOOKS

Castles in the Sand (a novel)
By Carolyn A. Greene, $12.95

East Wind
By Ruth Hunt, $12.95

Foxe's Book of Martyrs
By John Foxe
$14.95, illustrated

In My Father's House
By Corrie ten Boom, $13.95

Let There Be Light
By Roger Oakland, $13.95

Stolen from My Arms
By Katherine Sapienza
$14.95, photos

*Stories from Indian Wigwams
and Northern Campfires*
Egerton Ryerson Young
$15.95, illustrated, photos

Strength for Tough Times
By Maria Kneas, $7.95

The Hiding Place
By Corrie ten Boom, $10.95

The Light That Was Dark
By Warren Smith, $12.95

The Messiah Factor
By Tony Pearce, $12.95

DVDS

The Story of Anita Dittman
with Anita Dittman
$15.95, 60 minutes

The New Face of Mystical Spirituality with Ray Yungen
3-DVDs, $39.95 or $14.95 ea.

The Radicals
Story of Christian persecution
$19.95

The Reckoning
Documentary on WWII resistance, $19.95

CDS

Good News in the Badlands
with Bob Ayanian
Americana gospel folk music
$16.95, 19 songs

Introducing:
Canadian singer Trevor Baker
CDs: *It's All in Place*, $16.95
The Lonely Road, $16.95
Bring Me Back, $16.95

For a complete listing of all our books and DVDs, go to www.lighthousetrails.com, or request a copy of our catalog.

To Order Additional Copies of:

For Many Shall Come in My Name
send $12.95 plus $3.75 for 1 book (or $5.25 for 2-3 books) to:

Lighthouse Trails Publishing
P.O. Box 908
Eureka, MT 59917

You may order online at
www.lighthousetrails.com
or
Call or fax our toll free number:
866/876-3910 [U.S. ORDER LINE]
For international and all other calls: 406/889-3610
Fax: 406/889-3633

For Many Shall Come in My Name, as well as all books by Lighthouse Trails Publishing, can be ordered through all major outlet stores, bookstores, online bookstores, and Christian bookstores.

Bookstores may order through
Ingram, Spring Arbor, or directly from Lighthouse Trails.
Libraries may order through Baker and Taylor.

Quantity discounts available for most of our books.
International orders may be placed either by phone, online, through e-mail, or by faxing or mailing order form (see website).

For more information:
Lighthouse Trails Research Project
www.lighthousetrailsresearch.com

Visit Ray Yungen's website at www.atimeofdeparting.com.